CW00860046

There's no such thing as a Perfect Crime

A crime novel by

Andrew Hawthorne

Dedications

This book is dedicated to my son Jack who encouraged me to publish and who helped to design the cover.

I should also like to thank Joseph and Claire Docherty for their positive and constructive feedback.

Chapter 1

3:12 am: Sunday, 19 August 2018

The thief, a man of medium build, wearing dark clothing walked slowly towards what he hoped was his next target. He had the hood of his jacket pulled up over his head and his head down to hide his face from sight. He carried a small black backpack on his back which was perfect for his purpose.

When he reached the gate of the big detached house, he looked slowly in both directions along the street to make sure no one was watching him. Then, in an instant, he skipped inside the gate and crouched low against the other side of the small hedgerow. The air was very still, there was no wind or breeze to rustle the leaves of the trees and he could hear nothing other than the odd passing car on a distant road.

The house was in complete darkness as was expected; he had watched this house over the last three nights and there hadn't been any lights turned on which was a real give away. The lack of any cars in the driveway also gave him some confidence that the owners were still away but he would proceed with the utmost caution and leave if there were any signs of life. He had already abandoned two other jobs for this very reason and was not prepared to take any chances. He could see that there was a light with a PIR sensor above the main door and he guessed there would be another one at the rear of the property. The sensor would turn the light on in response to any movement it detected so he knew he would need to avoid its range when approaching the house. Thankfully he was far enough away from the entrance or the light would have turned on as soon as he entered the gate. Having made up his mind to proceed, he moved quickly around the perimeter of the property until he came to the dividing wall between the property and its neighbour. He followed the moss covered wall around the house until he reached the back garden and crept towards what appeared to be the kitchen window while being careful not to make any noise on the gravel path which led from the back door to further down the end of the garden.

Again, there were no lights on and again no noise coming from the property. With his back to the wall he crept slowly along the edge of house until he reached the back door. Being so close to the wall he had managed to avoid setting off the PIR sensor which was directly above the back door.

He removed his backpack and took out a small torch, turned it on and pointed it at the lock. It was a standard Yale lock which would be easy to open providing the owner hadn't put the internal snib in the locked position. *It was incredible how many people didn't do this simple thing.*

He put the torch back into the bag and then took out a pair of disposable plastic gloves, put them on and took a credit card size piece of plastic from his pocket and gently pushed it between the small gap between the door and the doorframe. Almost immediately he could feel the lock's mechanism move as it pushed softly against the internal spring. He slowly and firmly turned the door handle, the door opened and then it stopped dead. He put the card back into his pocket and put his left hand behind the door and felt the short door chain which was preventing the door from opening fully. He knelt down to his backpack and took out a very crude version of a crochet hook, which he had made from an old wire coat hanger. He carefully felt for the chain again and this time closed the door over just enough to let the short length of chain slacken. Using his little manmade tool which he held carefully between his thumb and index finger, he caught the end of the chain and slowly pushed it towards the end of the hasp. The bolt of the chain slipped out of the hasp and the door opened wide revealing a small kitchen. He put his tool in the backpack and quickly entered the dark space.

From the stale smell of the air he could tell that the house had not been occupied for a few days.

He closed the door over and listened carefully for any sounds coming from inside the house. *Silence.* He took his torch from his backpack and switched it on. He shone the little metal torch around the kitchen and quickly found the doorway which led to the rest of the house. Once in the main hallway he spotted the stairs and slowly climbed up in search of the master bedroom. Having reached the upper landing he tried the first door and found the bathroom. The next door led to a single bedroom and the next door opened up to a larger room with a big bay window overlooking the front of the property. He switched off his torch and slowly let his eyes adjust to the darkness.

There was some light coming from the street lights to the front of the house and so he was able to see his way around the room without any additional light. He moved towards the tallboy which was facing him and saw a small jewellery box sitting there. *Too easy,* he thought and allowed himself a small smile. This was his favourite moment – opening the box to see what little treasures awaited his inspection.

The lid had a small gold coloured clasp which he opened carefully. *No point breaking it*, he thought. Immediately he could see the gaps from where certain rings had been removed but there were plenty left. *She has probably taken some with her on holiday*, he thought. Most of the remaining items appeared to be cheap costume jewellery with large imitation stones and he was slightly disappointed. He carefully selected two or three of the rings which were either gold or platinum; they weighed more than the cheap stuff and were also engraved with a small hallmark so he knew they would be worth taking. He then started to sift through the chains and other items of jewellery in the box. Having decided to take a few of the chains, he came across an old brooch which was quite heavy and looked to be of good quality. It had a large green stone in the centre of a rather ornate setting with various swirls and twists imprinted on either side of the gem. *This is more like it*, he thought. He put it in his backpack along with the other items that he had selected. He then had a quick look through the drawers of the tallboy but found nothing else worth taking. There were a few gents' watches in one of the drawers in the bedside cabinet but his buyer would not take them off his hands. It was also too risky for him to try and sell them online so he left them there. He then systematically went through the other drawers looking for any cash or other valuables left behind but found very little of any interest.

Satisfied that there was nothing else of any value in the room, he quickly searched the other bedrooms and then decided to leave. He left the way he had entered the house - by the back door, and sneaked around the side of the house until he reached the front gate. After a quick look in both directions he was on his way, walking slowly as if he was in no hurry to reach his destination. Once around the corner, he crossed the road and walked on down the short hill towards his car. He had deliberately parked the small Toyota in a quiet car park with no houses or buildings overlooking it. Once safely inside his car he took a deep breath and drove off, satisfied that he had not made any mistakes.

Chapter 2

7:00 am: Monday, 20 August 2018

Peter Macdonald woke up at 7 a.m. to the sound of his radio alarm which he set religiously every night before going to sleep. As always, he quickly put on the clothes he wore the night before and went downstairs where Sally, his four year old Cocker Spaniel, was waiting to greet him before going on their daily morning walk. As usual Sally was excited to see her master and as usual Peter reprimanded her for jumping up on him as he entered the room. Sally had been a rescue dog who had been abandoned by her previous owner; something which Peter could not understand. He loved dogs and had wanted one when he was a child but that had never been an option for him. Peter had been taken from his mother when he was three years' old and as far as he was concerned she had abandoned him. He spent most of his childhood in foster care and latterly was put into full time residential care by the local authority. When he was fifteen years old he was told that his mother had died due to a drugs overdose but by then he didn't care. He hated her and didn't attend the funeral. He was offered counselling at the time but never participated in *their pointless mind games*. So, now at the age of 28, it was just Peter and his dog Sally.

Peter and Sally left by the back door of his modest three bedroom house in the east end of Dumbarton and followed the same route that they took every morning. Sally had picked up the scent of another animal that she wanted to sniff and pulled hard on the lead, eager to hunt down this strange smelling creature that had scurried along the path during the night.

'Good Morning,' Peter said to another dog walker as they passed each other. This was also a regular event as they saw each other on most mornings at the same place and same time on the cycle path. Peter didn't know his name but always offered a friendly smile to be polite.

'Not so nice today, looks like rain', said the man smiling and looking down at Sally who was actively sniffing the rear end of the wee Highland Terrier who appeared to be mesmerised by Sally's sweeping tail as it wagged from side to side in continuous motion.

'Yes, it's supposed to brighten up later though...see you later,' Peter said as he gently pulled Sally away from her little friend and continued on the walk.

Further on, a female jogger approached them. She had headphones plugged into her ears and nodded and smiled at Peter as she ran past him. Peter had seen her before on her morning run. She was petite with short brown hair and despite her reddened face from her exertions, she was clearly very pretty. He turned around to take another look and admired her slim profile from the back. *Perhaps one day he would work up enough courage to ask her out,* he thought to himself. And on that happy thought he walked on with Sally leading the way home.

Fifteen minutes later, Peter and Sally arrived back at their house. Peter cleaned Sally's paws with the towel, which was left lying at the back door for that purpose, and then prepared her breakfast; the usual mix of tinned meat and kibble. It looked awful but Sally didn't seem to mind. As Sally scoffed her food, Peter made tea and toast and put on the television as was his daily ritual. Having brought himself up to date with the latest local and national news, courtesy of BBC Breakfast, he went upstairs to get showered and dressed. Half an hour later, he came back downstairs to find Sally lying in her basket, content after her exercise and meal. Sally looked up and saw Peter in his blue suit, white shirt and tie and knew that this meant that she was going to be left in the house alone again. Her head dropped down to the floor, her big brown eyes looking forlornly at her master as he prepared to go to work.

'You're in charge Sally,' Peter said in jest. 'Don't let anybody in and if the postman knocks the door make sure you bark as loudly as you can!'

Sally's ears perked up at the sound of her name but then relaxed again as she realised she wasn't expected to respond. Peter picked up his briefcase and left the house by the front door. He could see Mrs Baker, a neighbour from across the road heading out to work. She locked her door and walked briskly in the direction of her car, a blue Ford Focus which looked a bit faded as a result of years of good Scottish weather beating down on it.

'Hello Helen,' Peter shouted over to her as he walked towards his own car; an immaculate black BMW that was 5 years' old but still looked as good as the day he bought it. 'Back to the grind again?' he asked.

Mrs Baker stopped in her tracks, looked round and seeing Peter, she shouted back 'Oh, hi there… in a bit of a rush…didn't see you. Yes, back to work as usual.'

'Yes, unless we win the lottery?' he joked.

'I wish,' she replied as she ducked down into her car, started the engine and drove off.

Peter drove away from his street and joined the main road. He turned left towards Glasgow and joined the flowing stream of traffic, all heading to their various places of work; some listening to their choice of music and others, like Peter, listening to the radio. Peter always listened to the local radio station and was keen to hear the latest news on the recent crime wave which was getting the local press and radio very excited. At 8.30 a.m., the newsreader led with a story about an explosion at a chemical plant in Paisley and although the incident did not occur in West Dunbartonshire, where the local radio station was based, the smoke from the fire was drifting across the River Clyde and affecting homes in Clydebank. The radio reporter said, 'The Police have advised residents to remain indoors and to keep all windows and doors closed.' *Better avoid that area then,* Peter thought to himself and continued to listen to the rest of the news.

Chapter 3

8:30 am: Monday, 20 August 2018

Detective Inspector Claire Redding was sitting at her desk reviewing a number of unsolved cases which she had inherited when she took on her new role in the Criminal Investigation Department in Dumbarton. Her most recent promotion to the position of Detective Inspector came after her involvement in taking down a drugs gang which had established itself in Milngavie; a relatively well-off town on the outskirts of Glasgow. She had been based in Maryhill Police Station at that time and had previously spent two years in uniform in Rutherglen before applying for a place in CID. Her quick rise through the ranks had already been noted by the Chief Constable and he and other senior officials were keeping a keen eye on her progress.

Her new caseload included a number of house break-ins which her predecessor, DI David Anderson, had failed to progress. At his retirement party, he had reluctantly admitted to her that he was at a loss to solve any of the reported burglaries, all of which had one thing in common; the thief had not left any trace of evidence behind. There were no forensics to be tested and no clue as to the identity of this villain, who was not only very good at avoiding arrest but was always very selective in the items that were taken. She continued to read through the small stack of files convinced that DI Anderson must have missed something.

'Any joy?' asked DS O'Neill as he entered the room. Detective Sergeant Brian O'Neill was 40 years' old, six feet tall and was beginning to gather some excess baggage around his waist. He had been based in Dumbarton for some time and although he wasn't the brightest copper she had come across, his local knowledge had already been very valuable to her.

'What...eh, no...not yet Brian', she sighed. 'I can't believe forensics found nothing! Nine house break-ins and nothing! It's unheard of...'

'That's what DI Anderson said...poor bugger, just what he didn't need. And right before his retirement!'

'Brian,' she paused and took a deep breath, 'was he any good...DI Anderson?' she asked tentatively, knowing that Brian had worked with him for at least six years and they had become very good friends.

'Yes,' he said quite sharply. 'He was and...well, if you don't mind me saying, I don't think you have earned the right to question his work yet. He was a bloody good detective, very thorough and made a lot of arrests in his time so don't go thinking you can stroll in here and suggest otherwise. It broke his heart to leave without solving these crimes. Even you have to admit we are up against a real professional this time. Most criminals around here always make a mistake after a while, but not this guy.'

'What makes you think he's a guy?' she asked, ignoring his outburst. 'Why not a woman or are we not smart enough to be professional criminals!' she retorted half-jokingly.

'Okay, it was just a slip of the tongue,' he replied a little sheepishly. 'The problem is we have absolutely no evidence to go on!'

'Well, I'm going to keep reviewing these files until something jumps out at me. What are you working on?' she asked.

He grinned, 'I've had a report of a break-in at one of the pubs in the town centre. If it's okay with you, I'll take Colin with me. Apparently the owner thinks there is something on CCTV that might be useful, shouldn't take too long.'

'Okay, see you later,' she said, and went back to reviewing the case files without looking up to acknowledge his departure. *CCTV,* she thought*, I wonder if DI Anderson thought to check if there were any CCTV cameras in the vicinity of these break-ins.* She jumped out of her seat and ran out into the corridor to see if Brian was still around but he was gone. She went back into her office and looked out of the window. Detective Constable

Colin Kennedy and DS O'Neill were getting into one of the unmarked cars used by CID. *Oh well, I suppose it can wait,* she thought and returned to her desk.

Chapter 4

6:30 am: Thursday, 23 August 2018

The alarm went off at 6.30 a.m. DI Redding turned over, leaned towards it and hit the off switch. She lay there for a few minutes, gathering her thoughts, preparing mentally for the day ahead. She was quite excited as she genuinely thought she had a bit of a breakthrough with the burglaries. DI Anderson hadn't checked any of the CCTV footage and although it was most unlikely that there would be any footage kept on disk from the earlier burglaries there was a small chance they could get something from the most recent ones which hopefully had not been overwritten or deleted. She had asked DS O'Neil and DC Kennedy to identify all known premises with cameras near the last four burglaries and today they would visit as many of them as possible to see if the criminal had inadvertently been captured on camera. She accepted that it was a long shot, but at the moment they had nothing else to work on and at least she could tell her boss, DCI Tom Morrison, that they were following a new line of enquiry. He was getting increasingly concerned about the lack of progress being made and had made it abundantly clear that he had high expectations of Claire, given her reputation. She was desperate to please him and although her team had cleared up a few other cases in the very short space of time she had been there, this was clearly the top priority. It was only a matter of time before there would be another burglary and the pressure would be on. She didn't believe it was possible to break into a house without leaving any evidence behind but so far she had to admit there was nothing obvious.

She got out of bed and went into the bathroom. She splashed some water on her face and went back to the bedroom to put on her running gear. She didn't run every morning but today she felt good. The weather forecast, if correct, suggested there would be some cloud but little or no rain. P*erfect for running,* she thought to herself.

In the kitchen, she drank a cup of water, did some light stretching and made her way out of the door. She switched on her IPod and chose her favourite playlist which comprised an eclectic mix of blood pumping tunes, perfect for jogging. She had a number of favourite routes and today she would run along the cycle path which was not far from the small flat that she was renting. Sensibly, she was waiting for her previous flat to sell before looking for another to buy. It was currently under offer but she wasn't prepared to take any risks before the deal had been done; she had heard too many horror stories about buyers withdrawing at the last minute.

Halfway along her run she passed by the man with the lovely wee black and white Cocker Spaniel. She had seen him a few times since she had moved into the area. She smiled, acknowledging him as she passed. He looked nice but *he was bound to be married or be with someone – all the good ones were,* she thought! She had had a few boyfriends but nothing too serious; her job often got in the way of personal commitments, which for some reason seemed to irritate them. *But, she was only 29 and had plenty of time to find the right man,* or so she told herself. She checked her watch and was pleased to see that she had reached just over halfway. *The second half was always easier. I'm feeling good so let's up the pace a little, she said to herself.* She started to jog a little faster and was soon back in her flat, slightly out of breath but pleased that her level of fitness appeared to be improving with every run.

Chapter 5

8:00 am: Friday 24 August 2018

They always met in the dealer's home; a small council flat in a rundown housing estate on the outskirts of Dumbarton. Most of the other flats in the block were empty and their doors and windows had been boarded up by the Council to prevent any vandalism to the interior of the properties, which was not a good look. However, it was the sort of place where people minded their own business, they didn't talk to their so-called neighbours and certainly didn't pry or ask any nosy questions.

The thief had arranged to meet his dealer at 8 a.m. sharp, and was on time. As always, he had done his homework in preparation of the meeting but was particularly interested in the value of brooch as he was now sure that the large green stone was an emerald. The dealer had been a jeweller before he was sacked for stealing from his last employer so he would know if the stone was real or fake.

He knocked on the dealer's door, which was on the ground floor to the left as he entered the close. The dealer looked through the peep hole and proceeded to release the two steel bolts which he had installed at the top and bottom of his door. He then unlocked the five lever mortice lock with its small but strong steel key and opened the door.

'Hello Jim, come on in', the dealer said as he ambled back towards the living room at the end of the hall.

Jim was the name he had given the dealer to use. He closed the door and pushed both bolts into position. He didn't turn the key of the door as the bolts were more than strong enough to hold back any unwelcome visitors. As a further precaution, the back of the door had been reinforced with steel plates, so no one was getting though that in a hurry. The dealer was not taking any chances and Jim liked this.

'How are things Bill?' Jim asked, as he entered the front room.

Bill had his back to Jim and was in the process of closing the venetian blinds at the window. 'I'm fine, take a seat', he said pointing to the settee. Both men sat down.

Jim took a small bag out of his jacket pocket and passed it to Bill, who immediately opened it and carefully poured the contents onto the small coffee table which he had placed in front of his chair.

Bill promptly inspected the chains and rings, carefully examining the hallmarks with his jeweller's loupe, a single eye magnifying glass, which he had also stolen from his previous employer. 'Well, well, well...what do we have here?' he said out loud. He picked up the brooch and carefully examined it for hallmarks and then looked closely at the gem. He smiled. 'This is beautiful,' he said 'but it might be difficult to move given its age and style'.

'That's your problem', said Jim. 'So, what's it worth?' he asked casually, trying to hide his eagerness to find out.

'I'll give you a hundred for the chains, two fifty for the rings and another four fifty for the brooch. Eight hundred quid in total, how's that?' he asked.

'Come on Bill', said Jim. 'The brooch's worth more than that on its own'.

'Maybe, but it won't be so easy to sell,' Bill said almost apologetically.

'Well, you can always remove the emerald and sell it separately,' replied Jim.

'I never thought of that. It would be a shame to ruin the brooch though, it's a cracker. Okay, I'll give you a grand for the lot. Deal?' asked Bill, and offered his hand to Jim.

Jim hesitated and then shook Bill's hand. Jim knew it wasn't worth arguing with the dealer and he needed the money.

Bill went through to the small kitchen and came back with a wad of cash which he counted out in front of Jim. Jim took the cash, thanked Bill and stood up to leave.

'It's been a pleasure doing business with you,' said Bill and led Jim to the door which he opened and stood back to let him pass. 'Come again,' Bill chuckled, and closed the door.

Jim could hear the lock turning and the two heavy bolts being slipped back into place. He turned and walked out of the close and turned right. As a precaution, he had parked his car two streets away and walked off quickly in that direction. When he got to his car, he decided to head off to town as he had some urgent business to take care of.

Chapter 6

8:30 am: Friday 24 August 2018

Claire drove her private car into the staff carpark which was located at the rear of the Police Headquarters in Dumbarton. As she got out of the vehicle she looked up at the concrete monstrosity of a building which was her current place of work. The Overtoun building, which had been built in the early 1970's to accommodate the newly formed 'L' Division of Strathclyde Police, was in a poor state of repair and needed extensive restoration. Claire noticed that some of the external cladding was missing and wondered if it had fallen or had been removed. *Hopefully the latter,* she thought to herself as she quickly entered the building.

'Good morning Brian', she said as she entered the CID room.

'Morning boss', he said, briefly looking up at her as she entered the room and then returned his attention to the monitor.

Claire looked around the office and asked, 'Where's Colin?

'He's already out and about looking at some CCTV footage from the wee off-licence in Old Kilpatrick.' He turned to look at her and said 'If it's okay with you, I'm going to head out and check the CCTV at the Car Wash on Cardross Road, just in case it picked up anything from the Oxhill Road break-in.'

'Yes, that's fine,' she said.

They had agreed that they would go out and check each premise with CCTV on their own to save time and if there was anything at all worth reporting, to bring back a copy of the recording to the station for further examination.

'Just keep in touch and let me know if you find anything. I'll be out and about as well, so call my mobile. Oh, and can you contact Colin and remind him to do the same please?'

'No problem,' he said as he got up to leave the office.

She saw him take out his mobile phone and start talking as he walked down the corridor towards the exit. Having had a quick look at the files again she decided to try the Dumbuck Crescent break-in. There was a small Keystore at the corner of Glasgow Road and Greenhead Road which also had a cash machine out front. She thought that she might need to contact the bank to get CCTV footage from the cash machine but she also hoped that the store had its own cameras in operation. It was a long shot but she knew they needed to be thorough and eliminate all possibilities. As she was just about to leave, her desk phone rang. She went over to her desk and answered it. It was DCI Morrison. He wanted an update on any progress and didn't sound very happy. She explained that they were looking at CCTV to assist with their enquiries and assured him that she would provide an update if there was any break through with the case. On that rather unnerving note, she put down the phone and headed out to the car park.

On her way to the Keystore she received a call on her mobile which automatically connected to her car's sound system. She recognised the phone number and said 'Hi Colin, what's up?'

'Good news boss, I think we've got something worth looking at. The night before the break-in in Old Kilpatrick, there's a man walking by the house, he stops and then has a good look before carrying on again. It's difficult to see if we can get a good look at his face as the screen here is tiny, but Brian said you wanted to know if I found anything at all, so...'

'Good work Colin, get a copy of the recording and head back to the station. I'm just about to check out the Keystore on Glasgow Road and should be back within half an hour or so,' she said.

'Will do', said Colin and hung up.

At last, she thought, *let's hope we have something to go on.* She pulled her car into the small access road which led to the rear of the premises and parked her car. The shop was around the corner so she needed to walk around the front to enter the store. She quickly took down the details of the cash machine as she passed it and then entered the small doorway leading into the shop. The shopkeeper was serving a customer as she entered, so she stood back until the customer left.

She approached the shopkeeper, took out her Police ID, showed it to him and introduced herself. She explained why she was there and quickly established that there was nothing of any value recorded on the shop camera. The shop did have a camera but it was in a fixed position and was focussed on the till area. Given that the till was behind the serving counter, which was offset from the entrance, there was no chance that any view of the outside of the premises could be caught on the CCTV. However, the shopkeeper was able to confirm that there was a small camera hidden in the cash machine but he didn't have access to the images and couldn't confirm if the camera was only activated when the cash machine was used. She thanked the shop keeper for his help, left the shop and returned to her vehicle feeling a bit disappointed. However, she was keen to see what Colin had found and drove quickly back to the station.

Chapter 7

9.25 am: Friday 24 August 2018

As DI Redding entered the staff carpark she could see DC Kennedy entering the building. She quickly parked her car and with a spring in her step walked briskly to the CID room.

'Hi Colin, let's see what you've got then.'

Claire walked towards his desk to look at his PC, where he had plugged in a USB pen drive and was in the process of scrolling down the list of files until he saw the one he was after. He clicked on the file and the media player software opened automatically. He clicked play and the video began playing. He fast forwarded to the correct time and then let it play.

'There he is,' he said as the man came into view. 'That's the house. See how he stops, has a good look and then walks on'. He turned to look at her, awaiting her response.

'Yes, certainly looks a bit suspicious, but I couldn't see his face', she said. 'Can you stop it just as he turns towards the camera, we might have a side on view which can be enhanced?

He started the video again and stopped just at the moment when the man on the screen turned.

'There,' she said. 'Hmm, I'm not sure we have enough but let's send the file to the Technical Team and see if they can improve the quality of the image. It's a pity the camera is so far away from him but I suppose we're lucky to have caught anything on camera at all. Did you check the footage on the day of the burglary to see if the camera picked up anything?'

'I had a quick look at the off-licence but didn't see anything. I've got a copy of the files here though so I can have a proper look now. It'll take a bit of time; we don't know what time the break-in took place so there's a lot of video to get through.'

'Okay, good and well done', she said. 'At least, we've got something to go on but only if we can get a better look at his face! We don't even know if this is the guy so let's not get too excited yet.'

'Yes boss,' he said and went back to his screen to look at the video.

Chapter 8

11:17 am: Friday 24 August 2018

Later that morning Brian returned to the office to report that he had struck a blank at the Car Wash. Claire updated him on the image they had taken off the CCTV in Old Kilpatrick. Colin was still staring at his screen and was beginning to look a bit jaded.

'Anything?' Claire asked as she approached him.

'Not really,' he said. 'Just a man walking his dog and stopping briefly at the gate, it's hard to see if he's looking at the house or just waiting for his dog to move on.'

'Hardly a crime!' she said.

'Not unless it does its business and he walks on without picking it up!' Brian said jokingly.

'Okay, trust you to lower the tone. Let's review what we know so far and see where that takes us.'

Claire moved towards the wall with the large white boards where they had posted information on the crimes. The two men stayed in their seats but turned towards her. She pointed to the local map where they had plotted all the locations of the burglaries.

'So, we know that all of the burglaries happened in private houses in and around the Dumbarton area. We also know that he likes to break into houses where the owners are not at home – so presumably he's checking them out beforehand. Hopefully, Colin has found an image of him which we can use. Did you send that video onto the technical team?' she asked.

'Yes, but it's going to take a few days before we get it back. They're really busy right now and burglary does not merit the same level of priority as other more serious crimes,' he said slowly, anticipating a reaction.

'Tell that to the DCI!' she exclaimed and turned back to examine the board..

Colin looked at Brian and winked. They both knew she was under pressure to get results and clearly it was beginning to get to her.

Claire turned back towards her team. 'Okay, so he's working in the West Dunbartonshire area and we think he is operating in the middle of the night to avoid being spotted, so how he's getting from A to B? There's no public transport at that time so he must have his own car.'

'Good point boss,' said Brian agreeing with her logic.

'We also know that he can open most types of lock so what does that tell us? Has he done some time in jail? Has he trained as a locksmith at some point in his life or has a family connection, was his father a locksmith?'

She paused for a second, reviewing her thoughts and then continued. 'We also know he's very careful and has not left any physical evidence behind, so far. He's also very fussy about what he takes and often leaves other items of jewellery behind. Why?'

DS O'Neill sat up in his chair and said, 'We know he's careful, so perhaps he's only taking items which are hard to trace. Let's face it; we've not been able to get anything back from these burglaries so he must have a good fence.'

'That's right, so let's shake up all the known fences in the area and see what happens,' Brian suggested.

'What? Do you think they're just going to fall over and give us a name?' said Colin sarcastically.

Claire started to speak, considered what she was about to say and then continued. 'No, Colin's right, I think we need to be a bit smarter than that. Brian, can you produce a list of all known fences or dealers in the area and prepare a short list of those who you think are most likely to deal with jewellery? I'll speak to the DCI about authorising some overtime to allow us to carry out 24 hour surveillance on them.'

'Do you think that's likely boss? Colin asked. 'You know how tight budgets are these days.'

'Leave that to me Colin,' she said, knowing full well that it would be an awkward conversation. *If the DCI is serious about getting this thief he will need to put his money where his mouth is,* she thought.

'Right, what else do we have?' she said rhetorically. 'If we assume that he is the man in the CCTV then he would appear to be of medium build and height and as far as I can tell he is between 20 and 30 years old – it's hard to tell from the video footage but hopefully we'll know more when the technical team come back with the enhanced images. Okay, Colin, can you finish checking the Old Kilpatrick footage and then go have a look at the next place with CCTV?'

'Hardgate?' he asked.

'Yes, just off Roman Road, there's an RBS with a cash machine out front but we need to check if the bank has any other cameras which point outside. That reminds me, I still have to call the bank about the cash machine down at Glasgow Road.

'I'll do that boss,' said Colin helpfully. 'Just give me the details and I'll get onto them.'

'Thanks Colin. That leaves me to deal with the DCI!' she said as she left the office and headed towards DCI Morrison.

Chapter 9

11:30 am: Saturday, 25 August 2018

Claire was just leaving the exit of the Asda store in St James' Retail Park, with bags in both hands, when she felt something catch her feet and down she went.

'I'm really sorry,' the young man said helping her up.

She looked up and realised it was the man who walked his dog on the cycle path. At her feet was the wee Cocker Spaniel, excited and completely unaware of the chaos she had caused by running away from her master.

Peter looked down at Sally and immediately grabbed her collar and attached the lead. 'We were going to the vet and she bolted out the door before I could stop her. I should have kept her on her lead. I'm really sorry, are you okay?'

'No harm done,' she said looking down at her knees, which were a bit red but not bleeding. When she fell, her knees had bent forwards and she ended up practically kneeling on one of the bags full of shopping; good news for her knees but bad news for her shopping. She hoped it wasn't the bags with the eggs!

As she looked up, Peter suddenly realised who she was and felt a small lump form in his throat.

'What's her name?' Claire asked while getting up and rubbing her knees.'

'What...oh, it's Sally and I'm Peter. I've seen you jogging on the cycle path, I think,' he said.

'Yes, and I'm Claire,' she said offering her hand.

Peter shook her hand. 'I'm really sorry Claire. She's normally well behaved.'

'That's okay,' said Claire smiling down at Sally. 'You didn't mean it, did you Sally?'

Sally was excited and pleased that she was getting so much attention; her tail was wagging wildly and her mouth was wide open, as if smiling.

'Can I help you to your car?' Peter asked. 'It's the least I can do.'

'No thanks, I'll manage. Perhaps I'll bump into you again on the path?' she joked.

'Yes, of course, but not literally, I hope! I'll try to keep Sally under control next time.'

'See you then,' she said. Claire turned and walked away towards her car.

'See you,' he said and turned back towards the vets. *Go ask her out you fool*, he thought to himself. *You'll never get a better chance.* He turned to call out to her but she had disappeared out of sight. He looked around the car park and couldn't find her. Then he suddenly caught sight of her; she had been masked by the boot of her car while putting the shopping away and was now heading to the driver's door. He ran, pulling Sally with him. Sally soon caught up and overtook him but not knowing where he was heading she ran in the opposite direction and he almost went down as her lead crossed over his path. He reached the car and knocked on the driver's door window, slightly out of breath. Claire turned with a bit of a fright and then realising that it was him opened the window. Before she could say anything, he said 'I know this is going to sound a little weird but would you like to go out... for a drink, tonight or... another night when you're free?'

Claire was visibly taken aback by his sudden forwardness and didn't know how to respond at first. She hesitated and then said 'Let me think about it. I have other plans tonight so...'

'Oh, I see,' said Peter, a little deflated.

Realising that she had put him off more than was intended, Claire said 'What's your phone number and I'll call you when I'm free?'

'Great!' said Peter, who was unable to suppress his inner joy. 'It's 0767 987 6543. Do you want me to write it down?'

'No, I'll remember it,' she said and drove off.

'But what if ...you don't', Peter said as the car pulled away.

He wished he had not been so impetuous now. *Why didn't I ask for her number in return? Was she just being nice when she said she would think about it? Oh crap,* he thought. He looked down at Sally and said, 'I think I might've blown it! Come on, let's get you back to the vet!' They headed back towards the large Pet Store, which conveniently had a full veterinary clinic upstairs. As soon as Sally realised where they were going she started to pull on the lead and drag her feet. 'Come on girl,' said Peter who bent down and scooped Sally up off the ground with both hands and then marched off towards the store.

Chapter 10

12:15 pm: Sunday, 26 August 2018

Claire was sitting in her kitchen when her work mobile phone rang. She was still wearing her pyjamas even though it was almost lunchtime. She quickly looked at the screen of the small phone and tapped the green button to accept the call. 'Hi Brian, what's up?'

'There's been another burglary boss. A call just came in from a Mr Graham residing in 224 Smollett Street, Alexandria. He says the back door was open and some jewellery taken but no damage or any other sign of a break-in. Sounds like our man again!' he concluded.

'Yes, it does. Let the station know that I will attend this one in person and I'll meet you there in about half an hour?'

'Will do, see you there,' he replied.

Claire quickly went into her bedroom to get dressed. Her hair was a bit of a mess so she brushed it and put on a hat to make it less obvious that she hadn't showered that morning.

When she arrived at the house, she could see that DS O'Neill was waiting for her in his car. They both got out of their cars at the same time and walked down the drive to the front entrance. The door opened before they rang the bell.

Mr Graham, an elderly gentleman, slightly balding and looking rather tanned from his recent holiday had been anxiously awaiting their arrival. He saw them enter the driveway from his front room window and immediately went to the door.

DI Redding and DS O'Neill briefly introduced themselves, showed their identification and entered the house. After chatting to Mr Graham and his wife in the front room of the house, and having taken a full statement of the items which had been stolen, the two police officers went to the back door to inspect the point of entry.

'No sign of a forced entry,' said DS O'Neill. He put on a pair of disposable gloves, opened the door to check for any obvious sign of entry from the outside but couldn't see anything. 'Nothing', he said.

'Okay, let's get the SOCO in here to check for any finger prints, hairs, etc., and maybe we'll get lucky this time,' she said.

They went upstairs to look at the bedrooms. Everything looked in place, unlike some burglaries where drawers had been emptied onto the bed and tossed aside.

They entered the master bedroom and DS O'Neill immediately approached the little jewellery box which lay open on the tallboy. He looked inside and saw that a number of items had been left in the box. 'It's him alright, look at all the stuff he's left behind. I've never known a thief to do that; they normally toss the lot in a bag and scarper.'

DI Redding was very quiet. She looked around to the bedroom to see if there was anything that could help them catch this thief. 'He's certainly a cool customer. Look at how tidy everything is. I bet he has gone through all these drawers but there's absolutely no evidence to show that he has been there.' It's no *wonder DI Anderson couldn't catch him,* she thought to herself.

They went back downstairs to where Mr and Mrs Graham were waiting anxiously.

'Anything?' asked Mrs Graham looking more upset than she was when they first arrived.

DI Redding shook her head, 'I'm afraid not, but I will ask SOCO to...'

'What's SOCO?' asked Mr Graham looking rather agitated.

'Sorry, it's a Scenes of Crime Officer who specialises in gathering any forensic evidence at a crime scene. They will probably want to take samples of your hair and fingerprints to eliminate them from any others that are found in the house so don't be alarmed. If we find anything which does not fit, we can run a search on our database of known criminals in the hope we get a hit. Is there anyone else living in the house?

'No, just us, the children moved out a few years ago,' said Mrs Graham.

'And do you have any pets?' asked DS O'Neill?

'No, why do you ask?' asked Mr Graham, looking a little bemused by the question.

'They usually leave lots of hairs lying around which makes the SOCO's job that bit more difficult,' he explained.

'Ahh,' said Mr Graham nodding his head slowly.

'Oh, please try not to disturb anything in the master bedroom and around the backdoor before the SOCO gets here. We wouldn't want to disturb any evidence, would we?' DI Redding said as she turned to leave.

'What about insurance?' Mr Graham asked.

'When we get back to the station, we'll log the crime and issue a case number, which you will need to put on your claim form together with full details of the jewellery that was taken. Do you have any recent valuations as that will help to speed up your claim?'

'It's been a while,' said Mrs Graham. 'The brooch that was taken belonged to my mother. She left it to me in her will; I had it valued shortly after the funeral, must have been about 10 years ago. It was worth quite a bit back then so must be worth a fair amount now. Not that I really care about the money. I'd much prefer to have the brooch back, it means a lot to me,' she said as tears began to well up in her eyes. Mr Graham put his arm around his wife to comfort her and the two Police Officers took this as their cue to leave.

'Brian, can you call HQ and get a couple of officers down here to knock a few doors and ask if any of the neighbours have noticed anything suspicious over the past week? Oh, and see if there are any CCTV cameras around here? Colin can look into that tomorrow. I'll call in SOCO and update the DCI.'

'Sure, and nice hat by the way, bad hair day?' he said with a big grin on his face.

She laughed 'You don't miss much, do you Brian? See you later.' She looked up and down the street once more before turning towards her car. *So much for a quiet Sunday*, she thought as she drove back to the station to complete her report.

Chapter 11

9:00 am: Monday, 27 August 2018

DS O'Neill was sitting at his desk chatting to DC Kennedy about the latest break-in when DI Redding entered the room. She looked happier than usual and DS O'Neill, who was good at noticing these things, was wondering why she was looking so pleased with herself.

'Hi boss,' Brian said with a grin on his face, 'you look like you're the cat who got the cream.'

'Do I?' she said, smiling to herself as she sat down at her desk. She had called Peter last night and they had agreed to go out for a drink. Nothing formal, just a few drinks in the local hotel to get to know each other. She was both excited and a little scared at the thought of it as it had been a while since her last date.

'Well,' said DS O'Neill, 'spill the beans, what's making you so happy?'

'None of your business and don't be so bloody nosy!' she said pretending to be upset but failing badly.

'Must be a man,' said Colin joining in on the fun. 'Who is he, do we know him?' asked Brian.

'What is this, a Spanish inquisition, and what part of *none of your business* don't you two understand?' she said.

'Definitely a man,' said Brian, now enjoying her meagre attempts at putting them off.

'Right, that's enough; we've got work to do. Brian, did we get anything from the door to door enquiries yesterday?'

'No, nothing at all; no one saw anything or anyone acting suspiciously.'

'Great,' she said sarcastically, 'Colin, can you check any CCTV in the area?'

'Yes boss', he said.

'I don't suppose we have the SOCO report back yet?' she asked, looking at Brian.

'No, not yet' he said. 'Way too early for that...did you get authorisation for the 24 surveillance on the dealers? I have the list here.' He stood up and passed the printed sheet to the DI.

She glanced down at the list. 'Yes, I've got the warrants but the DCI wants us to try daytime observation first and see if we get anywhere. Thankfully, there are only four of them so we'll just need to take turns watching them. However, the good news is that we can focus on this case and nothing else; the DCI has decided that anything else that comes in will be passed to DI Stern's Team to deal with until we catch this thief.'

'Bit of a waste of time if you ask me,' Colin said. 'Chances are we'll never see him during the day, are you sure you want us to waste our time doing that instead of following up on other leads?'

'What other leads?' she asked, showing her annoyance.

Brian interjected before Colin got himself in deeper trouble. 'What about the image we sent to the Technical Team? Has that come back yet?'

'No, but good point, can you chase them up Brian? It would be really good if we could see what the guy looks like.'

'If it's him,' said Colin, feeling a bit miffed about being cut-off by the DI.

'True,' Claire replied, 'but it's all we've got until we get the SOCO report back. So it's back to the dealers.' She looked down at the list. 'Okay, Brian and I will take the first two on the list. Colin, can you pick one of the other two and start the surveillance after you've checked out the CCTV. If you find anything let me know and we'll review the plan but for now we have nothing else to follow up so let's get to it.'

'I'll take William Rowatt,' Brian said getting to his feet. 'Bill used to be a jeweller so he's top of my list'.

DI Redding looked down at the list and said, 'I'll take Jack Nairn'.

Colin went over to her desk and looked at the list. 'Okay, I'll take David Harold.'

The three officers left the station and went off in their cars.

Chapter 12

6:30 pm: Monday 27 August 2018

After spending most of the day in her car watching the dealer's house for any activity, which turned out to be completely futile, Claire was ready for a long soak in her bath before getting ready to go out. She had been thinking about it all day and had decided that she wasn't going to speak about her work on the first date. I don't *want to put him off before he gets to know me,* she thought.

Peter had been to the gym before going home but had allowed plenty time to shower and get ready. Sally knew something was up as he had broken from his usual routine. He decided to take Sally for a longer walk than usual before going out in the hope that she would be tired out and would just sleep while he was out. He didn't like leaving her in on her own at night and although he paid a dog walker to take her out during the day, he still felt guilty about it.

Peter arrived at the hotel first. He ordered himself a drink and found a quiet table in the corner of the lounge area. The bar area was always slightly busier than the lounge and thankfully there wasn't any football on the TV so it wouldn't be too noisy.

When Claire came in, she paused and looked around to see if he was there. He immediately stood up and waved to get her attention. She was looking prettier than ever and had clearly made an effort which pleased Peter. She had let down her short brown hair that was normally tied at the back which really suited her. He hadn't really noticed before but her eyes were aqua blue; she really was stunning. After briefly sharing some pleasantries, he went to the bar to get the drink of her choice – Gin and Tonic.

When he came back with her drink Claire thanked him and asked, 'Who's looking after Sally?' She was keen to start the conversation on something familiar.

'She's on her own tonight,' said Peter, 'I took her a big walk before I went out so she will be good for a couple hours or so; she will probably sleep most of the time but she wasn't pleased that I was going out'.

'What do you do with her during the day or do you work from home?'

'I sometimes work from home but when at the office I pay a dog walker to take her. It's a great service; they come and collect her from home, take her a big walk with other dogs and bring her back, happy but exhausted.'

'That's good, she's a lovely wee dog,' said Claire.

'I take it you've never had a dog of your own?' asked Peter.

'Nope, my parents were not pet lovers.'

'Do you still live with them?'

Claire smiled at the thought, 'No, I have my own flat now. What about you?'

'I have a small house in Dumbarton East, which I share with Sally.' he said carefully avoiding any reference to his parents.

'Are you from Dumbarton?' she asked gently probing a little further into his background.

'No, I'm a Lanarkshire boy. I got a job in Glasgow and moved here; it's a short commute and house prices are low,' he said by way of explanation.

Claire avoided asking about his work as this would inevitably lead to him asking about her work.

'What about you?' he asked. 'Where are you from?'

'Newton Mearns,' she said 'in the south side of Glasgow.'

'Ah,' said Peter, 'that explains it.'

'What?' she asked, somewhat confused by his remarks.

'Sorry, what I mean is that you are quite well spoken compared to the majority of folk around here,' he said.

She nodded and took a sip of her drink. 'You are quite observant,' she commented, 'And, by the way, so are you…well-spoken that is.'

'Thanks,' he said, 'I've had to work on it.'

'Oh, really, why?' she asked interested to find out.

'My job.' he said. 'I stuck out like a sore thumb when I first started. Most of the folk I work with come from a middle class background like you so I decided to change my speech to fit in better.'

'But why,' she said. 'Obviously you were good enough to get the job in the first place so why change?'

'It was my choice; no one said anything but I slowly became very aware of it. I, eh…' He was about to say that something else but held back as he didn't want to start talking about his childhood just yet. 'Anyway, that's enough about me, what do you do for a living.'

Now it was her turn to change the subject. 'Let's not talk about work tonight, it'll only bore you and put me in a bad mood.'

'Oh, okay', said Peter feeling a little awkward but keen to keep the conversation going. 'What do you in your spare time, I know you like jogging, anything else?'

The conversation got easier after that and after a couple of drinks they were chatting freely and enjoying each other's company. When it was time to go they got up and left the hotel together. Peter offered to walk Claire home but she politely declined. They agreed to go out again for a meal somewhere and spend a bit more time together. Claire gave him her number and after Peter had kissed her on the cheek, she turned and headed for home.

When Peter got home, he was greeted by Sally who was pleased to see him. He got the lead and took her out for her last walk of the day before bed. As he walked he replayed the date over in his head. *Could have been worse I suppose but there was that strange moment when I mentioned work and she cut me off dead. I wonder what that was all about!*

When Claire got home, she kicked off her shoes, put on the telly and slumped onto the couch. She had decided that she really liked Peter and wanted to see him again. *Could he be the one,* she thought to herself and giggled out loudly surprising herself. She fell asleep on the couch and woke up startled by noise from the TV. *Oh Lord,* she thought. *What time is it?* She looked at the clock and saw it was after 2 a.m. She got up and went to bed half asleep still thinking about Peter.

Chapter 13

8:30 am: Tuesday, 28 August 2018

Claire had instructed her team to meet in the station to review the case and plan the day ahead. As she arrived, the two men were chatting and laughing together and then stopped abruptly as she entered.

'What's up,' she asked as she took off her jacket and sat down at her desk.

'Nothing much, Colin was just telling me about something he saw on the CCTV camera at the BP petrol station,' said Brian.

'Related to the case?' she asked. 'I thought I told you to contact me right away...'

'No boss, it's not connected but it was hilarious though. This old guy clearly out of his head on booze or drugs or something, staggers up the station, attempts to lean against a post to light a cigarette, misses the post and goes down sideways. You remember that scene on 'Only

Fools and Horses' when Del Boy tries to act cool at a bar and falls sideways through the gap, well it was just like that but even funnier.'

They all started laughing at the thought of it. 'Was he okay?' asked Claire.

'Who?' said Colin, trying to control himself.

'The drunk,' she said as if it was obvious what she meant.

'I think so. He got himself up and carried on as if nothing had happened! You couldn't make it up, it was so funny.'

'Okay, thanks for that Colin,' she said bringing the hilarity to a close. 'So, do we have anything new, Brian?'

'The images came back from the Technical Team late last night. I would've called you but it turned out to be a waste of time. There's a shadow right across the face of the suspect so there is no way of identifying him, if indeed it was him.' He showed the DI the enhanced image and she nodded in agreement with his conclusion.

'Back to the drawing board then,' she said. 'Did anyone see anything worth reporting yesterday?' she asked, more in hope than anything else.

'Nope,' said Brian.

'Told you so,' said Colin.

'Okay, okay, it's early days yet and we still have the SOCO report to get back, so let's keep our fingers crossed. In the meantime I'm afraid it's back to daytime surveillance. Let's keep watching the dealers and see if anything crops up today.'

Having had their instructions, both men grabbed their jackets and left the room. Claire remained at her desk; she had a few emails to deal with before she went out and she had also received notice that she was required in court a week on Wednesday. She had been called to give evidence on a Glasgow drugs case which she had worked on before she started in Dumbarton. *I better let the DCI* know about it, she thought, and headed to his office.

She knocked the door and entered. DCI Morrison was sitting at his desk, speaking loudly on the telephone. He acknowledged her and waved her into the room. She sat down on one of the chairs facing him. He was in his late fifties but looked older than his years; his hair was greying at the sides and he was beginning to go bald at the top. As DCI, he had dealt with some of the most brutal crimes including manslaughter and the work had clearly taken its toll on him. Claire had been involved in a few manslaughter investigations but she knew that being responsible for the case was very different and that one day it was a pressure that she would need to deal with if she wanted to progress her career.

He finished his call and immediately asked for an update on the latest burglary.

'We're still waiting for the SOCO report, sir,' she said. 'The CCTV image of the suspect came back from Technical but I'm afraid it's useless. We've started surveillance on the dealers but nothing so far. I'll keep you informed, of course.'

'Of course…,' he repeated.

And before, he could continue, she interjected. 'I've been cited to give evidence at the Harris case. You know the one, I told you about it when I first started working here. I'll need to be in court next Wednesday and hopefully shouldn't take any longer than a day providing there's no delay.'

'Yes, the drugs case, okay. I suppose you have to go but keep the pressure on these burglaries. We really need some results soon.'

'Yes sir, of course.' she said and stood up and left his office. She went back to her desk to deal with some more emails before going out on surveillance again. She was beginning to wonder if Colin had been right. Daytime surveillance was turning out to be a fruitless exercise.

Chapter 14

12:30 pm: Tuesday 28 August 2018

Claire was in her car and was just about to bite into the homemade salad roll that she had prepared earlier that morning when her mobile phone started to ring. She checked the screen and saw it was DS O'Neill.

'Hi Brian, what's up,' she asked with a mouth full of food.

'Hello boss, is that you?' said Brian, in response to the muffled voice he heard on the other end of his phone.

'Yes,' she said, her mouth now clear of food. 'Just trying to eat my lunch, what's up?'

'I've just had a call from the station and apparently, earlier today a man attempted to sell a brooch matching the description of the one stolen from the Graham break-in to a pawn shop in Glasgow.'

'Brilliant! Do we have a description of the seller?' she asked.

'Don't know, that's all we've got for now. I want to go and interview the shop owner right away. Do you want to join me or are you happy for Colin to go?'

Claire ignored the question and asked her own, 'Why did the pawnbroker call the station?'

'Don't know… that's one of the many questions I'll be asking along with a request to see their CCTV. With any luck I'll recognise the bugger.'

'Okay, I'll come with you. Meet me back at the station in ten minutes and we can go together.'

'Good, see you then. Oh! What about Colin?' Brian asked.

'Let him know where we're going and why. He can continue to keep his dealer under surveillance for now but if you recognise the seller from the CCTV, we can call Colin and get him to keep our suspect under surveillance until we get back. With any luck we'll catch the bugger with stolen goods in his possession'.

'Sounds like a plan, see you back at the station boss,' he said, and immediately called Colin to tell him the good news.

Claire wolfed down the remainder of her roll and drove back to station as fast as she could without breaking the speed limits. She could only use the blue light in pursuit of a suspect or in an emergency but this didn't quite meet the criteria. As she arrived at the station, Brian was waiting for her.

'How did you get here so quickly,' she asked knowingly.

'Blue lights', he said without hesitation.

'But…oh never mind, she said. Right, where are we going?'

'Maryhill,' he said.

'My old turf…whereabouts?' Claire asked.

'It's one of the Cashbuster stores just off Maryhill Road, on Duart Street.' Brian replied.

'I think I know it,' said Claire.

'Great, let's go,' said Brian, smiling from ear to ear. Finally, they were chasing a good lead - the best part of the job as far as he was concerned. This was the reason why he joined the force and he was excited at the prospect of solving this one. *Wouldn't do his career any harm even if Claire would get most of the credit,* he thought to himself.

As they turned into Duart Road it was obvious there was nowhere to park near the shop so Claire drove further up the small hill and turned into a quiet lane. She parked the car and they both walked quickly back towards the pawnbrokers. When they entered the shop it was clear that this was a thriving business. The current financial climate of austerity together with the impact of universal credit had resulted in a resurgence of pawnbroker shops in areas like Maryhill, where levels of poverty were much higher than the national average.

Claire approached the shop assistant who appeared to be guarding the entrance to the premises and introduced herself. She asked to see the Manager and they were quickly escorted to rear of the premises and entered the back of the store via a secure door.

They were greeted by a tall thin man, about 60 years old with thick black hair with white roots, who introduced himself at Tom Finney, Store Manager.

'Hello,' he said. 'I've been expecting you.'

Claire showed her ID and briefly introduced herself and DS O'Neill. 'Thank you for calling in about the brooch. It's not everyone that would do that. Is there somewhere private we can speak and have a look at your CCTV recording?'

'Oh, didn't they tell you, the CCTV went down last week. I reported it to head office and an engineer has been requested but so far, no joy.'

The smiles vanished from Claire and Brian's faces.

'You have to be kidding,' said DS O'Neill.

'Sorry no, but I got a good look at the man and can give a detailed description if that helps.'

Claire smiled at Mr Finney and said. 'Of course, that would be great. Okay, let's find somewhere private and go over the details.'

The two police officers followed Mr Finney into a small office which was just about big enough to seat the three of them around a small tidy desk. Brian took a detailed statement from Mr Finney and he and Claire were confident that the brooch in question was very similar to the one that had been stolen on Sunday. It was Mr Finney who had served the man who tried to sell the brooch. He thought the man was acting funny; a bit nervous and agitated, and when he started to ask questions about the history of the brooch, the man took the brooch back and left the shop quickly. He immediately called the Police and the rest was history. Claire thanked Mr Finney for his assistance and diligence and asked if he would be willing to come into the station at some point after work to do an e-fit of the suspect. She explained that they no longer relied on artists impressions and that the e-fit technology was a far more accurate way of capturing the main features of a suspect. Mr Finney confirmed that he was happy to help and would be there at some point after six. He had seen e-fits of villains on the BBC's 'Crimewatch' programme and was quite excited at the prospect of being involved. The two police officers thanked him again and left the shop. Brian immediately called Colin and told him to keep an eye on Bill Rowatt's house and they would meet him there. Brian explained that they had been given a description of a man similar to Bill so they would want to question him, if he was still at home.

Chapter 15

2:30 pm: Tuesday 28 August 2018

When Claire and Brian arrived at Bill Rowatt's flat, Colin was waiting anxiously in his car. He immediately got out and met them at the close entrance.

'Has there been any movement inside?' asked Claire.

'Not that I could see, but the blinds have been closed since I got here so...'

'Okay, let's go and see if he's in then,' said Brian, keen to see if his memory of Bill Rowatt and the description given by Mr Finney were the same.

'Colin, you go round the back in case he tries to do a runner, and Brian and I will cover the front.'

'Okay boss, on my way,' said Colin as he strode through the close heading for the back garden.

Claire knocked on the door as loudly as she could and waited for a response but there was nothing. Brian tried knocking again, even louder this time and when there was no response he stooped down and looked through the letter box. He shouted Bill's name out a number of times but again, there was no response.

Before he started to shout again, Colin came back into the close looking a bit hot and bothered. 'I think you better take a look at this boss, there's evidence of a break-in in one of the bedroom windows at the back of the flat.'

'You're kidding!' said Brian and followed Colin out through the back door.

Claire decided to take a quick look through the front windows to see if she could see anything. The blinds were closed but there was a very narrow gap in the middle of the living room blinds and that's when she saw him lying on the floor, motionless; his right arm was twisted under the weight of his body which suggested he wasn't conscious.

Claire immediately ran to the back of the house where Brian was closely examining the damaged window. 'He's in the living room,' she said. He's lying in a heap on the floor. It doesn't look good at all. Call an ambulance!'

Claire went silent trying to think clearly about what to do next. 'Right Colin, get yourself in there quick and check for a pulse,' she said.

'But boss, won't he contaminate the crime scene?' Brian exclaimed.

'I don't care and we don't know for sure if it is a crime scene yet, it could be a heart attack or something.'

'Right, never thought of that.'

Colin carefully climbed through the small window frame as instructed. Brian called for an ambulance and after hanging up he looked at the open window. 'I'm glad you didn't ask me to go in. I'm not sure I'd fit through that window.'

Claire smiled at her portly colleague's attempt at humour and then headed back through the close to the front of the house. She peered through the window and could see Colin checking for a pulse and then putting his ear to Bill's mouth to check for any breathing. He looked up and saw Claire at the window and shook his head. Brian joined Claire at the front of the property and knew it was bad news from the look on her face.

Claire snapped out of her brief daze and took control again. 'Okay, we'll treat this as a suspicious death until we hear to the contrary from the pathologist. I want the SOC team to go over the house with a fine toothcomb. If he was our dealer then it's possible the thief has been here. I know he's been careful when breaking into houses but maybe not here. We can only hope!'

'Do you want me to call the DCI?' said Brian.

'No, I'll do it,' she said, resigning herself to the fact that the DCI might not be too pleased with the outcome.'

At that moment Colin came out of the front door. 'Like bloody Fort Knox in there,' he said. 'Had to find keys to get the door opened. No wonder the thief used the rear window to get access. Sorry boss, but I didn't have any gloves with me so it's likely SOCO will find my prints on the door.'

'Great, that's all I need!' said Claire and shook her head at the hapless DC.

'Did you notice anything suspicious?' asked Brian.

'What like?'

'Like large amounts of cash or jewellery! What do you think a dealer would have in there, you diddy.'

'But I thought the DI said it wasn't a crime scene!'

'No, I said we're not sure if it was a crime scene but given the circumstances I think we need to treat this as a suspicious death.'

'Oh, right,' said Colin feeling rather foolish.

'Okay Colin, start knocking doors to see if any of the neighbours have seen anything suspicious. I'll get a few uniformed officers down here to help with the door to door enquiries and let the DCI know what's happened.'

Claire walked over to her car to speak to the DCI in private; she didn't want Brian to overhear the conversation in case she got a hard time for ordering Colin into the flat which she was now beginning to regret.

To her surprise DCI Morrison was upbeat about the situation. He even agreed to let her take on the manslaughter case, if indeed that was the pathologist's opinion. The DCI's workload was full and given the progress she was making and the fact that the death could be related to their investigation he was of the view that it made sense for her to continue with both. And to her great surprise, he even offered her more resources; an extra Detective Constable and a Police Constable to assist with the gathering of evidence. When she ended the call she immediately went over to share the good news with Brian who was equally shocked but also pleased with the additional support.

After Bill Rowatt had been declared dead and the ambulance crew had removed the body, the SOCO team went in. Claire decided to call it a day; she couldn't do anymore at the scene and would need to write up a full report on the day's events for the DCI, so she left Brian in charge of the incident and went back to the station.

On route, she thought about Peter and decided that she would need to tell him that she was a police officer. She didn't like that awkward moment when he asked about her work and she ndidn't want to make it worse again this time round. The more she thought about it the more she wanted to be able to share some of today's news with him. The DCI was right, she had made progress and although she was disappointed not to have caught the dealer on CCTV she was sure Bill Rowatt was connected to the thief. She suddenly remembered that she had arranged for Mr Finney to come in after 6pm to do the e-fit. Hopefully there was no need now; he could be shown a photograph of the deceased dealer and hopefully give a positive identification. Was her luck finally turning! She couldn't wait to get back to the station.

When she arrived at the station, she was told that Mr Finney had been waiting patiently for her in the Reception. She went straight to the public Reception area and escorted Mr Finney up to her office. She explained that she was hoping an e-fit would not be necessary at this time and showed him a photograph of the suspect (now deceased) which she had taken on her phone before the body was removed. Mr Finney was confused at first but confirmed that Bill Rowatt was the man who tried to sell the brooch earlier that day. Claire thanked him for his assistance and advised that it was likely he would need to give evidence in court at some point in the future. This cheered him up and he left the office smiling; full of his own self-importance.

Claire, on the other hand, was feeling a bit jaded. She had just remembered that she was due in court the next day and hadn't done any preparation. *So much for drinks with Peter*, she thought and started to prepare the briefing for the DCI. She would prepare for court at home over a large glass of wine and then go to bed early so that she was fresh in the morning. She was a bit hacked off that she wasn't going to be around tomorrow to work on the case, especially now that they had a good lead to work on. *Hopefully the SOC team would find something useful at the Rowatt flat that would connect to the thief,* she thought. She decided she would call everyone into the office early next morning for a full briefing before she went to court. She called Brian and told him about the positive identification and the need for an early briefing in the morning. She then finished off the report for the DCI, sent it to his inbox, and went home.

Chapter 16

7:45 am: Wednesday, 29 August 2018

The next morning Claire had come in early to prepare for the briefing. When her two colleagues arrived at 8 am she quickly summarised the various actions needing to be done and then left Brian in charge to get on with them.

She was hopeful the pathologist report and SOCO reports would be available at some point that day given that they were now dealing with a potential manslaughter. When she arrived at the court she reported to the Sheriff Clerk's office and was directed up to Court No 6, where the case was being heard. There were two other Prosecution witnesses in front of her to be called so she knew she would need to wait a while. She had her laptop with her and intended to catch up with some emails but first she reviewed her notes for the court case.

She was still sitting in the waiting room at 11.13 am when she was finally called to give evidence. She put her laptop away and entered the court and was sworn in by the Clerk. After a brief period of questioning by the Prosecution Counsel and approximately 30 minutes of cross examination by the Defence, she was finally released. She had experienced much worse than that in other cases and was delighted to be able to get back to the station so quickly.

When she entered the CID office, Brian was studying what looked to be a SOCO report.

'Is that from Bill Rowatt's house?' she asked.

Brian looked up. 'Oh, hi boss, you're back early! No, it's the SOCO report from the Graham case.'

'Of course,' she said. 'I'd forgotten we were still waiting for that one. Find anything useful?'

'It appears they found some dog hairs on the bedroom carpet.'

'Really, I thought the Grahams said they didn't have any pets.'

'That's right, they didn't' said Brian.

Colin looked up, 'Remember there was some footage of a man walking a dog on the CCTV at Old Kilpatrick? Could be a coincidence but I also saw a man walking a dog on the CCTV sent from the cash machine at Greenhead Road. It didn't seem significant until now.'

'Certainly worth looking into, do we have a clear image of the man's face?' asked Claire.

'Not really, but I think the dog was a cocker spaniel, my cousin has one just like…'

'What colour? Claire said interrupting him. 'What colour was the dog?' she continued.

'Oh, eh, it's hard to tell as the image is in monotone but at a guess I'd say it's black and white. That's quite common for spaniels.'

Couldn't be, she thought. Claire paused for a few seconds. 'Okay, let's try and get a good image of the man before we take it any further. Colin, go over the footage again. Brian, can you get in touch with Mr and Mrs Graham and double check if they can explain the dog hairs.'

'Okay boss. How was court?' he asked.

'What…oh…okay…fine,' she said, clearly distracted.

'Are you okay?' Brian asked.

'Yes, I just have a lot of new information to process that's all. I'm more interested in getting the pathologist report on Bill Rowatt though. As soon as we know it's manslaughter the sooner I'll get additional resources to work this case. The SOCO report would also be useful right now.'

'Good point,' said Brian nodding in agreement. 'I'm not surprised we haven't got the SOCO report yet though. They spent hours going over the place last night. There's quite a lot of evidence to go through and we'll need more support to organise and sift through it once we get it all back.'

'I'm going to give the pathologist a call and see if he can confirm the cause of death. The official report can wait but I need to know what we're dealing with,' said Claire as she walked over to her desk still deep in thought.

Brian could tell something was bothering her but chose not to pursue it. Claire picked up the phone and called Dr Stott, the pathologist who had examined the body at the scene and who would probably carry out the autopsy. After a few minutes she was finally put through to Dr Stott who had just finished his examination of the body. He confirmed that Bill Rowatt had been strangled to death with what looked to be a belt or something similar. The exact time of death was always quite difficult to estimate with any level of true accuracy but Dr Stott was of the opinion that the temperature of body suggested that the time of death had been within two hours of the body being declared dead. She thanked him for his help and put the phone back in its cradle.

'It was definitely manslaughter,' she said out loud. 'Colin, what time did you arrive at Bill Rowatt's house?'

'About ten minutes after Brian called, why?' he asked.

'That was about 2 p.m. I think, just after we came out of the pawnbrokers. I'll check my phone,' said Brian reaching into his jacket pocket. He tapped on his phone and then quickly scrolled down his call log to check for the time. 'It was 2.01 p.m. to be precise,' he said.

Claire was now on her feet, thinking and speaking out loud so the others could join in. 'Okay, so the pathologist thinks the time of death was between 1 p.m. and 3 p.m. Colin got there at about 2.10 p.m. and didn't see anything so we can safely assume that it was sometime between 1 p.m. and 2.10 p.m. Assuming of course, that he was gone before Colin got there!' she said looking directly at Colin.

'I didn't see any sign of movement in the flat boss so I waited for you, as instructed,' Colin quickly interjected.

'Okay Colin, relax,' said Claire.

'Let's assume the thief was the killer and he had been in the flat before,' said Brian. 'Why break in through the window? Why not just knock the door and enter as before? If Bill was the dealer, there is no way he would have known that the thief was going to harm him.'

'Good point,' said Claire. 'But what if the Dealer was not in the house when the thief arrived? He would either have to wait for him, go away and come back or break in.'

'And assuming that it was his intention to kill the dealer before he got there, he decided to break-in round the back where no one would see him and lie in wait for the dealer to return.'

'That all sounds plausible,' said Claire. 'But why did the thief kill the dealer?'

The room fell silent. Eventually it was Brian who broke the silence. 'We don't know for sure if it was the thief. Do we? If Bill was up to his old tricks he could be dealing with any other number of criminals that we don't know about.'

'True,' said Colin.

Claire walked over to the office window and said 'Hold on let's take it back a bit. Did Bill have a car? And if not, how did he get to Maryhill? Did he take the train or bus? If so, let's circulate his photograph to the bus and rail services and see if anyone remembers seeing him.'

Claire was on a roll now and continued with her line of thought. 'Also, what if he tried to sell the brooch in another shop nearby? There's a load of pawnbrokers in that area, let's work our way through them all and see if any of them purchased the brooch.'

The room went silent again and then Claire sat down and said, 'Well, that's enough to be going on with for now. I'll let the DCI know it's definitely manslaughter so we can get a bit more support in here, we're going to need it.'

Chapter 17

6:30 pm: Wednesday, 29 August 2018

When she got home that night Claire was still buzzing with the excitement of the day's events. The pathologist report had come in late in the afternoon but had not really revealed much more that he had shared with her on the telephone. She had been told that the SOCO report would be on her desk first thing in morning, as it was now getting top priority due to it being a manslaughter case and she was really keen to see what it revealed about the victim and the killer. Both Brian and Colin had been busy trying to track down Bill Rowatt's movements and were making some progress. She had been so busy she hadn't stopped to think about Peter but now that she was home, she didn't quite know what to do about him. She was sure it was purely a coincidence that the CCTV had picked up the image of a man and dog and without any real evidence linking Peter to the crime she knew it would be completely unprofessional of her to jump to any conclusions at this time. However, she also knew she couldn't discuss the case with Peter which was what she really wanted to do. Maybe it was time to tell him about her job and see how he reacted. She decided to give him a call and see if he wanted to go out for a drink. She needed to relax a bit and a large glass of wine and some pleasant chat would certainly help. When she called Peter he was a bit hesitant at first, as he had been out all day and didn't want to leave Sally at home on her own which was understandable. He could hear Claire's disappointment in her voice and on the spur of the moment suggested that Claire could come round to his house for a drink instead of going out. She accepted his invitation and told him that she would bring a bottle of wine.

Peter looked down at Sally who was whining at his feet and said 'Guess who's coming to see us Sally, yes it's Claire. You like Claire don't you girl?'

Sally wagged her tail and barked, happy to have her master's attention again.

Claire arrived on time at precisely 8 p.m. She was wearing a different dress from before and was looking as pretty as ever. Peter hadn't really dressed up for the occasion and was now regretting not making more of an effort.

'Come in,' he said greeting her at his front door.

Claire could hear Sally barking somewhere in the back of the house.

'Sally's very excited to see you,' said Peter.

'Sounds like it,' said Claire smiling as she entered the small hallway.

Peter led her into his front room which was now very tidy by Peter's standards. 'I'll go and let Sally in now, I didn't want her running out of the front door as soon as it opened!'

'Of course,' said Claire.

Sally came bounding into the room, mouth open, tail wagging and immediately ran over to Claire who was now seated in the small settee which was placed in front of bay window to the front of the house.

'Sally, don't jump up on the furniture!' said Peter reading her mind. 'Down girl, come here, come!' Sally turned and could tell that Peter meant business and immediately went over to him and sat at his feet. 'Good girl,' he said and stroked her back. 'She'll be fine now, just a wee bit excitable to begin with.'

Claire smiled, looking down at Sally and said, 'Oh, I almost forgot.' She reached into her bag and produced a bottle of red wine.

'Thanks', said Peter, but you really didn't need to bother. I've got plenty of wine in the kitchen. I'll just get us some glasses' He got up, took the bottle and went through to the kitchen and came back with two large glasses full of wine.

After the first glass of wine was consumed they both began to relax a bit more and the conversation became easier. Peter was the first to mention work and Claire decided that she was ready to share.

'Okay, let's have a bit of fun. Before I tell you what I do for a living, try and guess,' said Peter.

'Oh, I have no idea,' said Claire happy to play along. 'Let me see, you can afford this nice house, you appear to be well educated...so your job must pay well. Am I right so far?' she asked.

'Not bad at all,' said Peter. 'Go on.'

'Okay,' she said as she looked around the room for further clues but could not any see anything. Her focus then moved onto Peter. 'You look quite fit, but your face and hands are quite pale which suggests you probably work in an office environment ...so an office job that pays well. I don't think you are in senior management due to your age and admin work doesn't pay enough, so that could mean that you must be some type of professional, like a solicitor or banker or a computer geek!'

Peter laughed at the last suggestion. 'Not bad,' he said, 'I'm actually a stock broker but don't work for a bank. I work for a small independent group of stock brokers based in Glasgow called Growth Enterprises, have you heard of us?'

Claire was pleased she almost got it. 'No, sorry...and now it's your turn,' she said interested to hear his perception of her.

Peter grinned. 'Okay, you're clearly well educated, probably in a profession, are you a teacher?'

'No, try again,' said Claire enjoying the game.

'Oh, I know, a librarian!'

Claire burst out laughing. So much so that Sally, who had fallen asleep suddenly jumped up wondering what was going on. Realising that everything was fine, she quickly settled down again.

'I guess you're not a librarian then,' said Peter. 'Am I close?'

'Nowhere near close,' said Claire.

'Oh, go on, put me out of my misery. What do you do,' said Peter feeling a little defeated.

'I'm a police officer,' she said looking at him straight in the eyes.

'No way,' he said.

'Yes way, I'm actually a police detective,' she said, happy that he hadn't gone completely silent on her.

'I should have guessed. Your powers of deduction are clearly far superior to mine. I'm in shock,' he said, sitting back in his armchair.

'You're okay with it then?' she asked tentatively.

'Of course I am,' he said. 'Why wouldn't I be?'

'Well, let's just say others have been less than enthusiastic,' she said feeling relieved that he now knew and clearly was not bothered by it at all. 'Anyway,' she said keeping the conversation flowing. 'Stockbroking... that must be fascinating?'

'Are you kidding? Compared to what you do stockbroking is a complete bore but you were right, it can pay well and I've been lucky recently. Some of my deals have paid out some big money to my clients which meant more commission for me.'

'What about your job though; tracking down criminals, putting them in jail, must be exciting?' he asked.

'It can be and today was one of those days, but for the majority of time it's a hard slog and can be quite disheartening when things don't go your way. I can't talk about specific cases though.'

'Hold on, I can't believe I've been so slow. You're not Detective Inspector Claire Redding? The detective who is investigating the recent spate of break-ins that the local press are getting so excited about?'

Claire blushed in confirmation that he was correct in his assumption.   'Yes, but as I said I can't talk about the cases.'

Peter, sensing the change in her tone, quickly responded, 'No, of course not. I didn't mean to suggest we should…sorry.'

'It's okay,' she said, realising that she may have been a bit over sensitive. 'How did you become a stockbroker?'

'Well, it's a long story but basically I had a bit of a rough time at school. I hated most subjects but mathematics always fascinated me and it was the only subject that I did well in. I went on to study statistics in college and was encouraged to do a degree in mathematics and economics by my college lecturer who said I had a real flair for it, and the rest is history as they say.'

'Your parents must have been really proud,' said Claire.

Now it was Peter's turn to go quiet. After a brief pause he took a deep breath and said, 'It's not something I share with many people, but my mother abandoned me when I was three years' old and I didn't know my father.'

Claire was stunned. 'I'm sorry, I had no idea, you're so norm...'

Peter cut her off. 'It's okay, I'm fine with it now but it did mess up my childhood for a while. I spent time with various foster parents before being admitted to a residential care home. I had a bit of an issue with discipline and authority back then. However, one of the positives of my depressing childhood was that I was encouraged to study and do well. I'm not so sure that would have happened if I stayed with my mother. She's dead by the way, a drugs overdose.'

Claire was now feeling terrible. 'I don't know what to say.'

'No need to say anything, it's all history now. I'm happy with my lot and you have a lot do with that,' he said looking directly at her eyes and holding her attention.

'Really?' said Claire.

'Really,' he said, and sat beside her on the small settee. He put his arm around her and they kissed; gently at first and then with more emotion and feeling. It was easy, no embarrassment, no awkwardness and both fully embraced the moment.

Chapter 18

8:30 am: Thursday, 30 August 2018

Claire started the morning briefing by introducing DC Joe Docherty and PC Bob Davidson to the team. For their benefit, she quickly summarised the information her team had gathered to date and outlined the evidence trail which had led to Bill Rowatt's house and the discovery of the body. She then went onto brief them on the current line of investigation and invited Brian to give an update on the calls to the other pawnbrokers in Maryhill.

Brian stood up and took centre stage. 'I've got some good news for a change. A man fitting Bill Rowatt's description tried to sell a brooch to one of the smaller pawnbrokers on Maryhill Road. They have some CCTV footage of him which I intend to check out after this briefing. If it was him then we'll know for sure that Bill Rowatt was the thief's dealer.'

'Good,' said Claire. We also know Bill didn't own a car so it's likely he made his way there by public transport. 'Do we have anything from the bus or train companies yet?'

'Not yet boss, so we will need to go and check their CCTV.'

'I'll do that boss,' offered Colin.

'Thanks Colin but I was thinking it was maybe a job for Joe, I'd have thought you'd be scunnered with looking at CCTV by now. How did you get on yesterday, did you manage to get a clear image of the man with the dog?' she asked.

'I got a good image from the cash machine on Glasgow Road but the image in Old Kilpatrick is useless due to poor street lighting. I checked the good image against the national database to see if there were any matches.'

'And?' she said, keen to know the outcome.

'No, nothing.'

'Okay, let me see the image when we're done here. I have the SOCO report to review. Bob, could you double check the evidence sacks and make sure everything is correctly labelled please? I want to go through the evidence and the report together but first I want to read the report quickly in case there's anything which needs to be followed up as a matter of urgency. After that I would like you to start organising all the reports, statements, etc. Oh, and highlight anything you think might be significant. It's always good for a fresh pair of eyes to look over the case.'

'Will do, boss.'

Brian, who had been listening in, approached Claire 'I managed to get a hold of Mr Graham last night. He confirmed they don't have a pet but he remembered that they had friends in the house a day or so before they went on holiday and their dog was with them so it's possible the dog may have wandered upstairs and went into the bedroom. He wasn't sure though.'

'Okay, well that might explain that one,' said Claire.

'Do you want to see the CCTV image of the man with the dog now?' said Colin, who seemed very keen to share his results.

'If that's all, then yes', she said moving towards Colin's desk.

Colin enlarged the image to fill the screen and there for all to see was a very clear image of Peter with Sally. Claire's heart jumped a beat.

'What's up,' said Colin. 'Do you know him?'

'Yes I do, and I doubt that he has anything to do with this case.' Claire said a little bit too quickly.

'We should probably interview him,' said Colin.

Claire hesitated but she knew Colin was right. 'I'll do it, but not here. I'll go to his home and speak to him informally for now. We don't have anything other than a CCTV image, it's hardly strong evidence.'

'Do you want me to come with you, boss? I don't mind working late,' said Brian.

'No, that won't be necessary,' said Claire quickly cutting him off.

'How well do you know him?' he asked.

'Look, he's just a friend of mine okay and I'm convinced he has nothing to do with this case but in the interest of being thorough I'll speak to him to make sure he has a solid alibi and we can move on. Okay!'

Claire knew she would need to speak to Peter about it at some point but how could she do it without offending him. There was no doubt in her mind that he wasn't the thief; he had a good job and didn't need the money, so what possible motive could he have to steal anything. That said, she knew she had to eliminate him from the enquiry and move on.

She returned to her desk and noted that Brian had already left to collect the CCTV footage from the pawnbrokers on Maryhill Road. Joe had also left, presumably on his way to check CCTV at Dalreoch train station which was close to where Bill lived. The others were busy carrying out the tasks allocated to them so she opened the SOCO report and started reading, taking notes as she went.

The first point of interest was that the SOCO team had found various pieces of jewellery and some cash hidden in the kitchen. They had managed to get some partial fingerprints from the bank notes which they had already run through the national database and found a match for Rowatt's prints, but no others which was disappointing. They also found a few human hairs on Rowatt's clothing, which did not match Rowatt's hair, and so the SOCO had sent it for DNA analysis. She knew they would also need to check that it did not match

Colin's DNA as he had been in such close contact with the body.

They also found some fibres from a jacket on the catch on the window and again she took a note that they would need to check against the fibres of Colin's jacket. She was beginning to regret asking Colin to enter the premises but she felt she had no choice at the time. Hopefully they would find some more evidence which could lead to the actual killer.

Having completed her initial review of the report, she started working with PC Davidson on examining the evidence sacks which he had now checked and confirmed were in order. She thanked him and asked him to organise all the statements and notes which had been taken from the door to door enquiries.

Just after 10 a.m. Brian came back into the office holding up a small pen drive for all to see. 'It was definitely him, boss,' he said. 'The CCTV footage shows Bill Rowatt with the brooch, clear as day.' He took the pen drive and plugged it into his pc. After a few minutes of searching he paused on the image of Rowatt standing at the counter with the brooch, both clearly visible.

Claire was pleased. 'Well done Brian. Now we know we're on the right track; Rowatt was definitely the dealer. The SOCO team found some cash and jewellery in Rowatt's kitchen and are currently running checks on some partial fingerprints that they managed to lift off the banknotes. I'm about to take a look at the jewellery to see if any of it came from one of the break-ins.'

Brian nodded in agreement. 'What about DNA? Are they able to test for DNA if they have fingerprints?'

'Don't know, said Claire. I'll take a note to ask that along with a few other questions I have for them. They did find some human hairs on Rowatt's clothing which will be checked against the national database. They might be Colin's of course, so he will need to provide some hair samples for elimination purposes.'

'What was that?' said Colin, hearing his name and suddenly showing an interest in the conversation.

'Oh, and they'll need your jacket as well, they found some fibres at the window sill,' said Claire.

'Great,' said Colin sarcastically. 'What am I going to wear in the meantime?'

Claire slowly shook her head at him and walked back towards her desk. She sometimes wondered how Colin ever managed to make it through the detective selection process and then she suddenly had another thought. 'Brian, do we have the time when Rowatt left the pawnbrokers?'

'Yes, it was at 11.05 am,' he responded.

'Have we finished checking with all the other pawnbrokers in the Maryhill area?' she asked.

'Almost, a couple of them didn't answer when we called them last night. I'll try them again now.' Brian paused for second and then continued. 'It's just a thought but what if Bill tried to sell some of his stuff to a jeweller as opposed to pawnbroker?

There are a few who buy gold for cash and might offer better prices than a pawnbroker.'

Claire was annoyed with herself for not thinking of that herself. 'Of course,' she said, 'I've been so focused on the brooch I forgot about the other items.'

'It wasn't just you, boss, we all did.' Brian said. 'I'll finish calling the pawnbrokers and then get on to the jewellers in that area. I doubt if he would be stupid enough to try to sell anything locally.'

'Thanks. I wonder how Joe's getting on with the CCTV at Dalreoch. I take it he's not called in yet.'

'Not yet boss,' said PC Davidson looking up from the large table where he was now sorting through the various interviews and reports.'

'I'll give him a quick call and find out.' Claire went over to her desk and called Joe from her landline.

'Hello Joe, it's Claire, anything to report?'

'There was nothing at Dalreoch so I went onto Dumbarton Central to check there. It occurred to me that he might have gone into town first before going for a train.'

'Good thinking,' said Claire.

'I've only just started to look through it but I'll call in if I find anything. It's a busier station than Dalreoch so it's not so easy to pick him out from the crowd.'

'That's fine. Take as long as you need and keep in touch.'

'Will do,' he said and went back to looking at the CCTV on the monitor in the back of the small office at Dalreoch Station.

Claire returned to studying the SOCO report and started going through the evidence sacks which PC Davidson had organised. She managed to cross reference some of the jewellery to other break-ins in the area including some carried out by the thief. This would be useful when appearing in court as it would help establish the link between the thief and the dealer and connect him to more than one crime, which was important for the purpose of sentencing. Of course, she needed to catch the thief first and still didn't have any solid evidence which led to his identity, unless of course the hairs found on the body belonged to someone other than Colin.

About an hour later, DC Docherty called in from Dumbarton Central. He had spotted Bill Rowatt getting on a train to Edinburgh at 9.54 a.m. According to the timetable, the train would have been due to stop at Hyndland at 10.12 a.m. where Rowatt would have needed to get off to connect to a train to Maryhill as it was on a different line.

Claire was delighted with the news and discussed the next steps with Joe. She wanted him to go to Hyndland station and check the CCTV there to confirm that Rowatt took the train to Maryhill station. Joe agreed and confirmed that he would leave his car in Dumbarton and catch the next train to Hyndland, view the CCTV there and then connect to Maryhill. He would then try to follow the route taken by Rowatt on foot to give a more accurate estimate of timings which was what they really wanted to know. He might also be able to establish which train Rowatt used to return to Dumbarton which was equally important as this would help to establish when Rowatt would have arrived home before being attacked.

At approximately half past twelve Colin announced that he was going down to the town centre to get some lunch. He asked Brian if he wanted to put a bet on at the bookies; apparently there was a big race on in Ayr that day and Colin had received a good tip on a young horse with a bright future. Brian declined but asked Colin to get him a couple of rolls and bacon on his way back. At this point PC Davidson also looked up and asked for the same.

'You lot will never reach retirement age if you continue to eat that stuff,' said Claire half-jokingly.

'I'd rather eat well and die young than eat the rabbit food you eat,' said Brian, referring to the very healthy but rather unappetising salad which Claire had just produced from her desk drawer.'

'Yeah, yeah, you say that now, but just wait and see if you still think that way when you're old and too fat to move,' said Claire as she stuffed her mouth full of tomato and lettuce.

Brian just shrugged his shoulders and went back to his work. He was happy with his weight and his health and didn't really care for others telling him how to live his life.

A few minutes later Joe called in with some more good news. He had found CCTV footage of Rowatt getting off the train at Hyndland and also getting on another train, presumably going to Maryhill. He also thought that he spotted him returning to Hyndland to change trains to go back to Dumbarton albeit the CCTV camera was a fair distance away, so he couldn't be one hundred percent sure it was him. Claire asked Joe to take the train to Maryhill and walk from there to the pawnbrokers on Duart Street, take a note of the time and then go to the second pawnbroker on Maryhill Road. If she had guessed correctly Rowatt would have tried the one on Maryhill Road first before going on to the one on Duart Street. She also asked Joe to take a note of any jewellers on the route, especially those advertising that they buy gold for cash. Joe, sensing the excitement in her voice, happily agreed to follow her orders. At first he hadn't been too happy being thrown into an investigation which another team had already started but the DI had given him a good task to get on with and he was pleased he was making so much progress on his first day. He had worked with both Colin and Brian before but this was his first time with DI Redding and was already impressed with the young DI's approach to the investigation. She was clearly on top of everything and had good instincts.

Chapter 19

11:30 am: Thursday, 30 August 2018

DC Joe Docherty had joined the CID three years earlier and was a little disappointed that he hadn't been promoted during that time. He was an ambitious young policeman and had sailed through the detective's examination with flying colours. However, he hadn't been given an opportunity to shine as a detective yet and was keen to please his superiors. So now that DI Redding had given him what appeared to be a pivotal role in the investigation he was a very happy man.

He was smiling when the train arrived at Maryhill station and as soon as he stepped onto the platform he took a note of the time. He then proceeded to the exit on his way to Duart Street with a real spring in his step. As instructed he took a note of any jewellers that he passed on the way. He would pay them a visit on the way back but first and foremost he would need to provide the DI with an accurate timeline of Rowatt's movements. When he reached the pawnbroker he noted the time and then proceeded to the one in Maryhill Road.

When he arrived at the second pawnbroker he took a note of the time and then headed back towards the station. As he was walking his phone rang to the tune of 'Simply the Best'; he wasn't a fan of Tina Turner but was a huge fan of Rangers FC, who had adopted the song during the glory years when they had won nine league titles in a row. However, those days were long gone and the league was now dominated by Celtic FC and had been ever since Glasgow Rangers had gone into administration. It had been a devastating time for all Rangers' fans but Joe kept the theme tune in his phone in the hope that those old glory days would return to his beloved club.

'Hello Brian, what's up?'

'Hi Joe, I've been in touch with one of the jewellers in Maryhill called Goldmans, who claim to have bought some gold chains from a man fitting Rowatt's description. Can you go and show them a picture of Rowatt to confirm it was him? Oh, and get a note of the time of sale and bring the gold chains back here. I'll send an image of Rowatt to your mobile to assist the identification.'

Joe recognised the name of the jeweller right way and confirmed he would go straight there as it was on his way back to the station. As soon as he hung up on Brian, his phone pinged to confirm receipt of an email with the image of Rowatt attached. *This was getting better by the minute* he thought to himself and strode off towards Goldmans.

Chapter 20

12:22 pm: Thursday, 30 August 2018

Colin came back into the office with a plastic bag containing the food which the team had ordered for lunch. He handed out the parcels in Greggs wrappers and sat down at his own desk preparing to eat his own unhealthy lunch. 'Any progress?' he asked no one in particular.

Brian nodded swallowing a large bite of his roll and finally mumbled, 'Hmm, yes. I got lucky with a jeweller in Maryhill. We'll also have a good idea of the timeline now as Joe thinks he saw Rowatt get on a train heading back to Dumbarton. We'll know more when Joe gets back.'

'Really,' said Colin before biting into a large pastry.

'What is that?' asked Claire, turning her nose up at the awful smell coming from the pastry that Colin appeared to be enjoying.

'I think it's cheese and onion', said Colin, taking another bite.

'I think I'm going to throw up,' said Claire and turned away from Colin's direction.

Chapter 21

12:38 pm: Thursday, 30 August 2018

DC Docherty entered the small jewellery shop and was announced by the ringing of a small bell which was fixed to a spring above the door. He looked around and then approached the young female shop assistant who was busy re-arranging some items of jewellery in one of free standing glass show cases to his left. As he approached she turned and asked if she could help him. DC Docherty showed his police ID and explained why he was there. Just at that point, an older lady came into the shopfront via a door at the back of the main counter.

'It's okay Jackie, I'll deal with this,' she said as she approached the young detective.

DC Docherty turned to face the voice which came from behind him. According to her name badge, she was Mrs Eileen Brown, Manager. She was about 50 years old and wore a smart white blouse with matching black skirt and waist coat. Her hair had been died dark brown to cover the grey but the roots were beginning to show which made it more than obvious to the young observant detective.

'It's about the gold chains you purchased recently. My colleague, DS O'Neill said he called. Did he speak to you?'

'Yes, but that was very quick; we only spoke about half an hour ago. He said he was from Dumbarton Police HQ and...'

'That's right but I was already in the area following up on a lead so here I am.'

'Right, I'll go get the chains then. I suppose you will want to take them away.'

'Yes, but before you do that, can you identify the man who sold them to you?' DC Docherty took out his phone and found the image of Rowatt that Brian had sent earlier. He showed it to Mrs Brown, who immediately confirmed it was the man in the photograph who had sold the chains.

'He seemed such a nice man,' she said staring at the image. 'Just goes to show you, never judge a book by its cover,' she said as she went into the back of the shop to fetch the chains.

'Here they are,' she said. I'll need a receipt for them though, just to keep our records straight.'

'Of course, what do you need me to sign?' said DC Docherty.

Mrs Brown went over to the till and brought back a small receipt book. She wrote the details onto the note and passed it over to him to sign.

'That's great,' he said. 'I'll need to take a short statement from you to confirm that Mr William Rowatt sold you these chains.'

'Oh, is that his real name then,' she asked.

'I assume he gave you a false name then.'

'He said his name was Peter Smith,' she said.

'Did you ask him for any identification at the point of sale?'

'No, but you can be assured that we will from now on, once bitten, twice shy,' she said bitterly, shaking her head slowly.

The young detective proceeded to take the statement and left the shop with the gold chains in a small plastic bag. He turned and headed back to the train station where he would take a look at the CCTV footage to confirm the time when Rowatt left Maryhill on his way back home. This would complete the timeline and hopefully help solve the crime.

After half an hour of searching, DC Docherty had found the information he wanted. Rowatt was caught clearly on camera getting on a train at Maryhill at 12.25 pm. Earlier Joe had thought he had spotted him on the CCTV at Hyndland getting on the Balloch train at 12.37pm, and so it all fitted together perfectly. He then checked the timetable which confirmed that the 12.37 pm to Balloch would stop at Dalreoch at approximately 1.07pm. So all he had to do now was time the journey from Dalreoch station to Rowatt's home. He decided to call DI Redding from the train and let her know what he had found so far.   As expected, she was delighted with the news and was happy for Joe to proceed to Rowatt's home.   Hopefully, this would tell her how long the killer had to enter the property and kill Rowatt before Colin arrived on the scene. She then asked Brian to meet Joe at Rowatt's and take the chains to the Graham's to see if they could give a positive identification on any of them.   This was all a necessary part of the chain of evidence if and when the case went to trial. Brian looked at his watch, checked the timetable and agreed to meet Joe at Rowatt's place in approximately 40 minutes which, according to his reckoning, would be about how long it would take, give or take a minute or so.

Chapter 22

1:35 pm: Thursday, 30 August 2018

Joe arrived at Dalreoch station and started walking towards Rowatt's flat. It took him approximately 12 minutes of walking at a reasonable pace to get there. When he got within 20 yards of the flat he saw that Brian was sitting in his car, waiting for him.

He opened the door of the Ford Mondeo and sat down beside his rather rotund colleague whose stomach appeared to be less than an inch from the steering wheel. 'Hi Brian, it's only a 12 minute walk from the station to here so that means Rowatt must have arrived here at about twenty past one, if the train was on time and assuming he came straight home.'

'Okay, that's good to know,' said Brian. 'Give me the chains and I'll go and visit the Graham's to get a positive identification on them. Where did you leave your car and I'll drop you there.'

'Thanks. It's down at Dumbarton Central,' said Joe and handed the small bag over to Brian who carefully put it in the inside pocket of his suit jacket.

Brian then drove off towards Dumbarton Central. Joe couldn't wait to get back to the station to share his findings with DI Redding. He was sure it was just a matter of time before they would find a key piece of evidence which would lead them to the thief and killer but he knew the difficult bit would be connecting both crimes. So far they only had circumstantial evidence, they needed some hard evidence to link the thief to the death but that was not going to be easy. Ten minutes later he was back in the office. Joe told DI Redding everything he had learned from the CCTV and the jeweller's shop.

'So, you reckon that Rowatt would have arrived home at approximately twenty past one which means we can now be pretty certain that the he was killed between then and when Colin arrived at the flat,' she said.

'Yes boss, but only if he went straight home,' he replied.

'That's good enough for me. We now have a very accurate timeframe of the killing. Bob, can you take a look at the statements made by the neighbours? I want you to focus on the issue of timing. How many were around at the time of the killing; did they notice anything unusual or different?'

'Will do boss,' he said.

'Okay, let's give this some more thought then,' she said turning towards the evidence boards. 'We now know that…'

Just then DCI Morrison entered the room and immediately approached Di Redding, 'Any progress?'

'Yes sir,' she said confidently. 'We have established a solid link between Rowatt and the recent spate of burglaries. We know he tried to sell some goods from the most recent burglary to a pawn brokers and jeweller's shop in Maryhill, we also know that he was killed between the hours of 1.20 pm and 2.10 pm, shortly after he returned home from his trip to Maryhill.'

'That's all well and good but what about the identity of the killer, any progress on that front?'

'We have hair samples from the deceased's clothing which have been sent to the lab along with samples of Colin's DNA for elimination. I'm waiting for the results and hopefully we will know later today if we have the killer's DNA or not. And now that we have an accurate timeline of the death we are searching through the door to door statements to see if any of the neighbours may have seen anything of relevance.'

'Okay, well let me know if you make any progress. I'm under pressure from the Superintendent to get results and he's not happy that I've put you in charge of the case so don't let me down.'

'No sir,' Claire said. She could feel her face reddening as he left the room.

The others in the room all turned back towards their work. The silence was deafening.

'Right, where was I,' said Claire, keen to change the atmosphere in the room.

'You were saying, *let's give this some more thought*, before the DCI came in,' said Joe.

'Yes, thanks Joe,' she said composing herself. 'So Rowatt has been to Maryhill, he's happy to have sold some chains and has some money in his pocket. So, what does he do now? Does he go straight home? He didn't have much time to do anything else so let's assume for now that he did go straight home. He enters the flat, locks the door, heads towards the kitchen where he hides his money, enters the living room where he is confronted by the thief who decides to kill him. Why? What is his motive? Is the thief scared that Rowatt will identify him? Why would he think that? Does the thief know that we are watching the dealer? Perhaps it's as simple as that! We know this thief is very careful so maybe he has been watching the dealer's flat before entering and has spotted us. He thinks that we are onto his dealer, he doesn't want to risk being grassed on so he panics and kills him.'

'Sounds plausible,' said Colin.

'It's a bit of a leap though,' said Joe. 'It's one thing being a common thief but committing murder and risking life in prison, well that's a whole different ball game!'

'I know,' said Claire. 'You're right. There must be something else. Something we're missing. Talking about missing, where's Brian?'

'Oh, he went to the Graham's House to get a positive ID on the jewellery,' said Joe. He should be back soon.'

'Of course, so he is, now let's get back to the grindstone and see what else we can find from the evidence we have gathered. Oh, and good work today everyone. We're making really good progress, despite what the DCI might think, so keep going and we'll get there.'

Joe walked over to the map. 'Boss, you know what you said about assuming Rowatt went straight home…well, it's just a thought but what if he got off the train at Dumbarton Central and then walked home via the town. He would just have enough time to get home for 2 pm. Why don't I go back to the Dumbarton Central and look at the CCTV footage. Now that I know what train Rowatt was on, it shouldn't take long to find out, then we'll know for sure. And if he did get off there, there's loads of CCTV in the Town Centre that we can use to trace his steps.'

'I'll go boss,' said Colin. 'I'm almost done here anyway and could do with some air.'

Claire thought about it for a moment. 'Why don't you both go? If he did get off at Dumbarton Central then we could save some time by having two of you on the ground. There's a load of CCTV cameras in the town so it could take some time.'

Colin looked at Joe and nodded towards the door. Joe nodded back and they both got up to go. Just as they were leaving Brian entered the office. 'Good news, the Graham's have confirmed that it was their chains which were sold at Goldman's,' he said grinning.

'I was pretty sure they would be,' replied Claire. 'Joe and Colin are off to Dumbarton Central to see if Rowatt got off the train there instead of Dalreoch.'

'Good idea, we need to keep the momentum going on this. You do know that he might have gone into hiding after the killing,' said Brian.

'Yes, and I think the DCI thinks the same, he gave me a bit of a hard time earlier.'

Brian looked at her and raised his eyes. 'Just what you don't need right now, eh!'

'Yes, but he was right. We don't have anything to identify the killer yet!'

'What about the hair samples? Do we have anything back from the lab yet?'

'Not yet, I've also asked Bob to examine the statements taken from the neighbours now that we have a more accurate timeframe.' She turned to Bob who was busy reading the statements. 'Well Bob, anything of interest?'

'So far, I've found one report of a man who was seen outside Rowatt's place at between 1.45 pm and 2 pm but the description pretty much matches Colin which is probably why it wasn't highlighted at the time.'

'Let's have a look,' said Brian.

Bob handed the sheet of paper to Brian who quickly read the content. 'Yep, that's Colin alright.'

Claire, took the paper, quickly read it and nodded in agreement. 'Okay, keep going Bob, hopefully you'll find something else. Brian, why don't we go and speak to the neighbour who gave the statement?'

'Can I grab a quick cup of tea first? I've a terrible drooth.'

Claire smiled at him. 'Of course you can. Oh, and make one for me while you're at it!'

'Huh, what did your last slave die of?' he said as he went off to make the tea.

Claire was going to reply with a sarcastic response and then thought better of it. She was beginning to warm to Brian's dry sense of humour.

Chapter 23

2:13 pm: Thursday, 30 August 2018

'That's him there,' said Joe pointing to the image of Rowatt on the screen. 'Just as we thought, he got on the 12.37 train to Balloch.'

Colin nodded and continued to stare at the screen. 'Right, let's take the quickest route to Rowatt's place and take a note of any cameras we see on the way.'

'What about the shops, shouldn't we take a note of any we think have cameras?' said Joe.

'Good idea,' said Colin. 'Why don't you walk the route and take a note and I'll stop at the shops on the way and check for any CCTV footage. We'll need to contact the Town Centre Management Company to access the street cameras but we can do that after we have identified and noted all the relevant camera positions.

Joe nodded in agreement, 'Sounds like a plan, let's go.'

Both men walk passed the Municipal Buildings which was on their left and then through the underpass heading towards the rear entrance to the Artizan Centre. This part of the town centre was run down and there were a few empty shops with some depressing 'For Let' signs hanging outside.

As they approached the High Street, there was a small Cash Generator Store on the left hand side of the walkway.

'They are bound to have CCTV,' said Colin and headed off towards the shop.

'See you later Colin,' said Joe and he continued on the agreed route taking note of any cameras along the way. He turned right as he entered the High Street and walked towards the west end of town. When he reached the end of the High Street he called Colin on his mobile.

'Hi Colin, I've taken a note of the CCTV cameras and now heading back your way. How are you getting on?' he asked.

'Nothing so far but I'll keep looking,' he replied.

Chapter 24

4:32 pm: Thursday, 30 August 2018

Claire and Brian got out of the car and headed towards the block of flats directly across from Rowatt's flat. They walked upstairs and knocked on the door of flat 3 which, according to the name plate, was the residence of Mr and Mrs Daly. The door was opened by an elderly lady with stringy grey hair which was thinning round the sides. She had dull blue eyes and was stooped over as if her head was too heavy to keep upright.

'Hello, I'm Detective Inspector Redding and this is Detective Sergeant O'Neill,' said Claire as she held out her ID. 'Are you Mrs Daly?'

'Yes, what do you want?' asked the old lady.

'Can we come in? We would like to speak to you about the statement you gave to PC Grey about the incident across the road.'

'Oh, that. Yes, I suppose so. You'd better come in then,' she said and turned back towards the hallway.

The two police officers followed her into the small flat. It was clear from the smell that it had been a while since the house had been properly cleaned. They could hear the television blaring in the front room. The old lady entered the room, picked up the TV remote control and turned down the volume.

'Come in and take a seat,' she said inviting them into the room and pointing to an old sofa which had seen better days. DS O'Neill sat down carefully, moving some cushions out of the way to allow him to fit neatly into the small seat. Claire sat down beside him.

'Did you know Mr Rowatt?' asked Claire.

'Who's that?' asked Mrs Daly.

'The man from across the road, the deceased,' said Brian, trying to be helpful.

'Oh him, not really, obviously seen him around but he wasn't the sociable type. Kept himself to himself, if you know what I mean.'

'I see,' said Claire. 'Do you recall the last time you saw him alive?'

'Now let me think? Must have been the day before he was killed I think...or was it the same day. My memory isn't what it used to be. Old age is a terrible thing you know.'

'Yes...and when you spoke to PC Grey you said you saw a man looking around the flats about 2 p.m. that day, the day he died?'

'Yes, that's correct, a very suspicious looking character. Was he the killer?'

'Did you get a good look at the man?' said Claire, deliberately avoiding the question.

'Oh yes, from that window there,' she said pointing to the large double window which looked out onto the street. 'I often stand up to stretch my legs and look out the window. Have a look for yourself, if you like.'

Claire stood up to see the view from the window. There was no doubt in her mind that Mrs Daly had a very clear view of the entrance way to Rowatt's block of flats. And even if there were cars parked on the kerb, the entrance to the close was clearly visible.

Claire looked round at Mrs Daly. 'Other than the man who was acting suspiciously, did you see anyone else approach the property around that time?'

'No, I don't think so,' she said.

'Okay, so you said it was about 2 p.m. when you saw this man. How can you be sure of the time?'

'Well, I had just finished watching the lunchtime news on the TV when I got up to stretch my legs.'

'BBC or ITV', asked Claire.

'ITV, I think!' she said unconvincingly.

Claire nodded at Mrs Daly and then looked over at Brian. 'DS O'Neill, do you have any other questions for Mrs Daly?'

'When you say the man you saw was acting suspiciously?' What do you mean by that?'

'It's hard to say really, he was standing about the gate looking left and then right as is if he was waiting for someone to arrive. He would look at his watch and then look around again.'

DS O'Neill nodded in agreement. *Colin was looking for someone…him and Claire.* Brian decided to take a different approach. 'You said that you like to get up and stretch your legs every now and then and have a look out of the window. Would you have looked out of the window before 2 pm, you know - when the adverts came on the telly or something like that?'

'How did you know that? I hate those bloody adverts! Yes I usually get up and have a look out the window during the adverts. Sometimes I make a cup of tea. Would you like one?' she asked, looking at both police officers.

'No thanks,' they both said simultaneously with comedic timing.

'Can you recall seeing anyone else earlier, did you see any cars coming or going?' asked Claire taking over the new line of questioning.

'No, I think there was a car but I can't remember how long it was there. I only remember because I hadn't seen it before.'

'Can you describe the car?'

I don't know the model if that's what you're asking,' she said, 'but it was dark blue, had four doors and one of them, eh, what do you call them again, oh yes, a hatchback.'

Claire and Brian both turned and looked at each other knowingly. It was Colin's car so no surprise there. Claire stood up to leave and thanked Mrs Daly for her cooperation.

Brian stood up and said, 'If you think of anything else please do not hesitate to contact the station. Here's my card,' he said and handed over a small business card to Mrs Daly who looked at it slightly bemused.

Both officers left the small flat and returned to their car. 'Well, we're not really any further forward are we,' said Brian as he buckled his seat belt and prepared to drive off.

Claire didn't respond; she was deep in thought. Something that Mrs Daly had said was bothering her but she just couldn't work out what it was exactly. She was going over the interview in her head and then it struck her. 'Brian, what time did you say that you called Colin to meet us at Rowatt's?'

'Eh, about 2 o'clock, I think!' he replied.

'Well there's no doubt that Mrs Daly saw Colin then,' said Claire.

'And identified his car,' he added. 'Just a pity she didn't see anyone else though. The killer must have avoided the front of the house and come in the back way. Makes sense I suppose. He certainly wouldn't want to be seen and we all know how careful he is!'

'Yes, I suppose so,' she said. 'Right, back to the station. Let's hope we have the results back from the lab.'

When they got back there was still no sign of the lab report and Colin and Joe were still out looking at

CCTV in the town centre so Claire decided she would deal with a few emails then go and see if Peter was at home.

Chapter 25

6:35 pm: Thursday, 30 August 2018

Claire had decided that she had to speak to Peter about the CCTV footage to eliminate him from the enquiry and so she headed to his house. As she approached his door she felt her stomach turn; she really was uncomfortable with doing this but knew it was better than letting another member of her team do it. She took a deep breath and rang the doorbell. She could hear Sally barking and then Peter's voice as he told Sally to be quiet.

Peter opened the door with one hand on the latch and the other holding back Sally. He smiled as soon as he saw it was Claire. 'Hello, come on in,' he said pulling Sally away for the door to make space for Clare to pass him in the small hallway. 'This is a pleasant surprise, what's the occasion?' he asked.

Before Claire could respond he ushered her into the front room, followed closely by Sally, who also wanted to say hello to Claire in her own special canine way. After patting Sally, Claire looked up at Peter and said 'I'm not sure how to say this but I'm actually here on police business.'

'Really, I am intrigued', said Peter looking slightly bemused. 'What about?'

'You know that I'm working on the burglaries?'

Peter nodded.

'Well, eh,' said Claire, trying desperately to find the right choice of words. 'One of our officers was reviewing some CCTV footage from near one of the crime scenes and happened to notice that you and Sally were caught on camera at the cash machine on Greenhead Road shortly before. I just need to ask you a few questions to eliminate you from the enquiry, that's all.'

'You don't think I'm the thief, do you?' he said half-jokingly.

'No, of course not, I just need to rule you out of the equation.'

'Okay, fire away,' he said.

Claire took out her police note book and opened it at a blank page. 'Can you remember what you were doing or where you were on the 27 August 2018 at about 10 o'clock at night.'

'Not specifically, but I usually walk Sally around that time of night.'

'And was that what you were doing that night?' she asked knowing full well that she would need a more positive response than the one given.'

'I think so, the only nights I have been out recently were with you,' he said smiling.

'I hate to push you on this but can you be more specific? Do you keep a calendar?

'Not really, I could check my work diary to see if that helps. Hold on a minute and I'll have a look'. He left the room and came back a few minutes later. 'Sorry, nothing specific I'm afraid.'

'Okay, assuming that you were walking Sally that night. Do you normally pass Greenhead Road?'

'Yes, it's on one of the routes that we walk,' he said. 'We go on the cycle path, turn right after the underpass and then down Greenhead Road towards the shop.'

Claire considered this and then went into her hand bag and withdrew a printed sheet which she passed to Peter. 'These are all the dates of burglaries which have taken place over the past year. Are you able to provide an alibi for any of those nights?'

'Crickey, that's a lot', he said looking closely at the list. 'I'll need to check my diary again if that's okay. It's possible I could have been away on business or on holiday. Hold on, yes, I was away on 16th and 17th June. I went to the Lake District with Sally. We went to a wee cottage just outside Windermere which allows pets. It's beautiful, have you ever been to the Lake District?'

'Yes, I went with my Mum and Dad when I was a toddler. I can't remember much about it though.

Anyway, I don't suppose anyone else can corroborate any of this?'

'The owner of the cottage could confirm that I was there, if that helps? Oh, and the landlord of the local pub. What's it called again? Eh, the Duck and eh...'

'Okay, thanks for that. If you give me the details of the owner we can check out your alibi. I am sorry I've had to ask these questions.'

'That's okay,' said Peter. 'Anyway if that's all finished with, have you had anything to eat? I was just about to start cooking when you arrived?

'No, I haven't but I really need to get home.'

'Oh', said Peter, 'this police business won't get in the way of us, well you know what I mean, our relationship?'

'Of course not', she said, and kissed him on the cheek as she passed him heading to the outside door. Just as she turned to say goodbye, her mobile phone rang. She groped around inside her bag until she could find her phone. 'Hello Brian, what's up,' she said. Her face turned white at the news she was given. 'Okay, I'll meet you there in five minutes.' She turned to Peter and just about managed to control the tears from running down her face.

'What's the matter?' asked Peter, realising something serious had happened.

'One of my colleagues has been found dead. I need to go now, sorry.' She turned and ran towards her car.

Chapter 26

7:15 pm: Thursday, 30 August 2018

The body of DC Joe Docherty had been found lying in a heap behind some large commercial waste bins in a lane not far from the town centre. A temporary marquee had been placed around the body to screen the scene from the public and the whole lane had been cordoned off with blue and white police tape. The pathologist was already examining the body when Claire arrived. DCI Morrison was standing beside Brian just outside the tent. Even he was looking a bit shaken by the sudden death of one of his officers and was unusually quiet when Claire approached him.

'Do we know cause of death yet, sir?' Claire asked.

'It looks like strangulation but we'll need to wait for the full autopsy to get that confirmed.'

Claire almost threw up at the thought of Joe's torso being cut wide open. Brian could see her reaction and took her aside. 'Are you okay? I have some water in the car.'

'No, I'll be alright. Just give me a minute will you. I'll be fine,' she said unconvincingly.

Brian stepped away from her and had a few words with the DCI.

Claire composed herself and went back to the DCI. 'Sorry sir, I'm fine now.'

DCI Morrison stared at the ground for a few moments before speaking. 'Look Claire, I've been thinking. This situation is getting out of hand and perhaps I shouldn't have thrown you in at the deep end so quickly. There's every possibility that both homicides are linked to the thief so I think it's best that I take over the investigation.'

'What, no, we're getting close. It's only a matter of time.'

'We don't have bloody time! You can still work the burglaries but everything must come through me from now on, do you understand?'

Claire looked down trying to hide the anger she was feeling, 'Yes, sir. I understand,' she said with gritted teeth.

'Good, now you go home and get some rest. I want a full briefing tomorrow morning at 8 am.'

Claire nodded and went back to her car.

Chapter 27

8:59 pm: Thursday, 30 August 2018

When Claire got back to her house she was still very angry and upset. She decided to go out for a run to relieve some of the stress. She got changed into her running gear and went out into the cool autumnal evening. She looked up at the grey sky trying to assess whether or it was going to rain and decided it didn't really matter; she was determined to run off some of the anger and then treat herself to a hot bath and a big glass of wine.

She ran all the way to Dumbuck Quarry via the cycle path and then decided to turn back towards home; it was beginning to get dark and there were very few people around. She wasn't frightened of the dark but preferred to avoid running into areas where there was little or no street lighting. When she reached the part of the path which ran parallel with Geils Avenue, she could see a man with a dog up ahead. As chance would have it, it was Peter and Sally out for an evening walk. She pondered cutting up onto Geils Avenue to avoid him; she didn't really want to talk about what had happened but then she thought better of it and ran slowly towards him. Sally recognised her before Peter did and started barking excitedly. Peter, who was in a complete daze at the time, was taken aback when he saw the runner approaching him. It was only when he finally recognised the runner to be Claire that he understood why Sally was getting so excited.

'Hello again,' said Claire as she stopped trying hard to catch her breath.

'Hi, I didn't expect to see you here,' said Peter. 'Are you okay, you know what with your eh, colleague being found. That must have been awful for you.'

'It was,' said Claire. 'And to top it all I've been taken off the case. Well not completely, just the homicide.'

'Oh, but I thought the cases were linked.'

'Yes, they are. It's just the DCI thinks I'm in over my head and wants me to focus on the robberies.'

'Seems strange, but then, what do I know about the police?'

They chatted for a while until Claire started to get cold. 'I'm really sorry but I'd better get home and get warm. There's a hot bath and a bottle of wine waiting for me.'

Peter laughed and gave her a big hug. 'On you go then, I'll give you a call tomorrow and maybe we can arrange to meet up at the weekend.'

'Yes, I'd like that,' she said and started jogging back towards her home.

Chapter 28

6:30 am: Friday, 31 August 2018

Claire woke up to the sound of her alarm feeling awful; the wine had helped her to get off to sleep but now she had a thumping headache. 'Oh God,' she said out loud. 'When am I going to learn?' She made her way to the kitchen and quickly swallowed a couple of paracetamol tablets with water. She then went to the bathroom to have a shower and stood under the hot water for at least 10 minutes as the paracetamol slowly worked its magic. Once dressed, she went downstairs for her usual breakfast of coffee and toast. As she sat at her small kitchen table sipping the hot steamy liquid she thought about what the DCI had said and decided that she wasn't going to let it get to her, she was going to go in and knuckle down.

She arrived at the station just before 8 am as instructed and was surprised to see Colin chatting to the DCI. Colin saw her first and indicated her arrival to the DCI by lifting his head and nodding. The DCI turned to Claire but instead of the usual morning greeting he said, 'I want to see you in my office, now.' He stood up and left the incident room. Claire looked at Colin seeking some form of explanation but he quickly turned away avoiding her stare. She took her coat off and hung it up on the coat stand in the corner of the room. She put her handbag in the bottom drawer of her desk and walked briskly back to the DCI's office completely confused by what had just happened. *What the hell had Colin said to the DCI to make him so upset?*

She knocked on the door and immediately went in to see the DCI who was sitting at his desk and looking very, very unhappy. Claire was a bit rattled by this and decided to stay on her feet. She could sense that she was about to get a telling off.

'Why didn't you tell me you had an image of a potential suspect?'

'What potential suspect?' she said automatically and then it suddenly dawned on her what this was all about. 'Oh, you mean, Peter. He's not really a suspect, he's...'

'He's your bloody boyfriend!' the DCI shouted.

'What, no he's...'

'So you are denying it now?'

'No, we are seeing each other but he's just a friend.'

'Just a friend? 'That's one way of putting it I suppose, but just a friend who just so happens to be caught on camera near the crime scene. Just a friend who has a dog when it's possible the thief you've been looking for also has a dog.'

'Wait a minute. What has Colin told you? We don't know if the thief has a dog or not.'

'Never mind what Colin has told me. What's pissing me off is that you didn't tell me. You're my DI for Pete's sake. I trusted you with this case. Gave you every opportunity and how do you thank me? You deliberately withhold information, important information, from me. And why, because he's a bloody friend! DCI Morrison was on his feet now, leaning on his desk. 'There's a dead cop in the morgue and I had to tell his family last night. I gave them my word that we would do everything possible to find the killer, track down every lead and what do I find out this morning, that you have been protecting your boyfriend.'

Claire realised that she had no defence. She should have told the DCI about Peter and now she was in real trouble. She took a deep breath and said, 'Look, I'm sorry. You're right to be angry but hear me out. I interviewed Peter last night. He has an alibi. I was going to tell you last night but I was rattled by the shock of Joe's death and...'

The DCI cut her off. 'What's his alibi?'

'Well I provided him with a list of the dates when the robberies took place and he was able to give a solid alibi for one of the dates.'

'And what about Rowatt's death, does he have an alibi for that?'

Claire froze. She hadn't even considered that Peter could be a killer, the killer.

'No, I don't know. I didn't ask,' she said knowing full well that the DCI was about to explode.

'You didn't ask,' the DCI said shaking his head in disgust. 'Well, I'll tell you what's going to happen now. I'm going to get him in here to question him properly and while I'm doing that I want his house searched from top to bottom. Tell Brian to get a search warrant. And as for you, you're off the case completely.'

'What! No, you can't. I'm...we're so close.'

'Listen Claire, you've had your chance and you've blown it!' There's plenty of other work for you to take on. You'd better hope that this Peter is not the killer or there will be hell to pay! Oh, and by the way what's his full name?'

'What?' It suddenly dawned on her that she didn't know. She had never asked Peter and now she felt like a complete fool. 'I don't know but I have his address so can quickly look it up on the system.'

'Unbelievable!' said the DCI. 'Get out of my sight!'

Claire was completely despondent. She turned to leave and then it suddenly struck her. 'What about Sally?'

'Who is Sally?' asked the DCI dismissively.

'His dog,' said Claire.

'Does Peter have any family who could look after it?'

'No, he doesn't have any family.'

'Well in that case the dog can go to the kennels until we know he's innocent.'

'I'll look after her,' said Claire, without really thinking through what it meant to look after a dog.

'What? You can't be serious. If you think I'm going to allow that, you have another thing coming!'

Claire was furious with herself. *Poor Sally*, she thought and *poor Peter. I've made things worse. I'm a bloody fool.* She left the DCI's office and went through to the incident room where Brian and the others were waiting for the DCI to show up.

'Hi boss, why the long face?' said Brian, who was completely oblivious to what was going on, unlike Colin who kept his head down.

'I'm off the case,' she said and before he could say anything, she added, 'I should have taken your advice. I should never have interviewed Peter on my own. The DCI wants him brought in for questioning and he wants you to get a warrant to search his house.'

Brian was stunned by the news and was unable to think of anything to say. At that point, the DCI came into the room and started barking off orders to all and sundry. Claire quickly collected her bag and coat and went back to the CID room where she was expected to do other work but she had no intention of doing so; she had to prove that Peter was innocent. Claire took out her notebook and looked through the notes of Peter's interview. She jotted down Peter's address and was about to Google it when she realised that she would need Peter's surname. She logged onto the Police server and quickly entered Peter's address. Within a few moments a name appeared – Peter

Macdonald. *Macdonald, so that's his name,* she thought. She called the number on her mobile phone but there was no answer so she left a message on the answering machine.

Chapter 29

9:15 pm: Friday, 31 August 2018

Peter was sitting at his office desk when Jackie, the Receptionist, called him to say that two Police officers had appeared at the reception and wanted to speak to him. He immediately got up from his desk and went to see what it was all about.

'Hello, I'm Peter Macdonald, what can I do for you?'

'Are you Mr Peter Macdonald who currently resides at 16 Silverton Avenue, Dumbarton?'

'Yes, what's this all about?' asked Peter.

'I'm DC Colin Kennedy,' he replied and showed his ID card to Peter who examined it and gave it back to the officer.

'We would like you to come to the station with us to answer a few questions about a number of robberies that have taken place in the Dumbarton area.'

'What? You must be joking. 'Am I under arrest?' asked Peter suddenly becoming concerned.

'Not at the moment although a warrant has been requested, we only want you to answer a few questions. However, we do have a warrant to search your home and would prefer that you give us access otherwise we will need to break in. I also understand that you have a dog so it would be better for all if you were to co-operate.'

Peter was stunned. 'But, I've already answered questions. Call DI Redding. She'll tell you. I've provided an alibi.'

'We're aware of that but we have a few other questions we want to ask and we would rather do that in the privacy of the station, wouldn't you,' said DC Kennedy looking around the small office.

Peter also looked round and noticed that the office had gone quiet; his work colleagues were all listening in with interest. 'I guess that would be best,' said Peter. 'Jackie, can you let the boss know what's happened. I'll be back as soon as I can. I'm sure it's just some sort of mix up.'

'No problem Peter, and don't worry, I'm sure you're right. I'll see you later,' said Jackie looking very concerned.

The two police officers looked at each other knowingly. There was no chance Peter was going to make it back to work today. Peter went back to his desk to get his jacket and then followed the two men downstairs where they had a car waiting for him.

'Is this necessary? I have my own car just round the corner. I could follow you back to Dumbarton,' he suggested.

'Sorry but you'll need to come with us,' the other policeman said.

Peter resigned himself to the situation and got into the backseat of the Police car. He wasn't overly concerned as he was sure Claire would sort it out as soon as he got to the station.

Chapter 30

9:55 pm: Friday, 31 August 2018

They arrived at Peter's home in Silverton Avenue where much to Peter's shock there were a number of police officers waiting for them. Peter got out of the police car and reluctantly opened the door to let the Police officers inside to begin their search. Sally was very excited at the sight of Peter and the other men entering the house and started barking.

'Do you have anyone who could look after the dog for you?' DC Kennedy asked.

'I don't have any family here if that's what you mean,' replied Peter.

'What about friends or a neighbour?'

'I could ask Mr Fraser at number 20, he's retired and has a dog of his own,' said Peter growing increasingly concerned.

'Okay, I'll send an officer to speak to him and if he agrees we'll give your dog to him to look after for now.   Failing that she'll need to go to the local kennels.'

'No, you can't do that!   She'll think I'm abandoning her; her previous owner couldn't look after her and she was put in the kennels!'

'Well let's hope your neighbour takes her in then.' said DC Kennedy. He instructed one of the uniformed officers standing outside the house to go speak to the neighbour and then escorted Peter to return to the police vehicle.

Peter felt sick at the thought of Sally being taken away. After a few minutes the police officer who had been speaking to Mr Fraser returned to the car. 'Good news, he's agreed to look after the dog until tomorrow. After that she will need to go to the kennels. Mr Fraser has asked about her food. Can you tell me where you keep it and I'll go and get it.'

'Thanks, that's a relief!' said Peter. 'It's under the kitchen sink. Oh, and thank Mr Fraser for me, will you?'

The police officer went into the house to look for the food. When the young police officer came out of the house he was not holding Sally's dog food, instead he had a small bag which he took over to DC Kennedy. DC Kennedy immediately made a quick telephone call and after a brief conversation, he took the small bag and approached the police car.

DC Kennedy sat in the backseat of the car next to Peter. 'Peter Macdonald, you are under arrest on suspicion of theft. You do not have to make a statement at this time but anything you do say may be noted and used in evidence. You have the right to see a solicitor which we can arrange when we get back to the station. Do you understand your rights?'

Peter was stunned by this sudden change in direction. 'Yes, but why, what's happened?' He looked down at the small bag. 'What's that?'

'You tell me, PC Brady found this bag in the cupboard under your sink? It appears to be full of jewellery. Been busy have you?'

'What? No, that's impossible. I've never seen that bag before!' Peter exclaimed.

'Save it for the DCI, he's waiting for you back at the station,' said DC Kennedy and instructed the driver to head to the station.

As the car moved away from the house, Peter could see Sally being handed over to Mr Fraser. He felt sick to the stomach; his head was spinning and he felt his heart begin to pound as his anxiety levels shot up beyond anything he had ever experienced before. He was totally confused. *How on earth did that bag get there?* 'It must have been planted,' he said out loud. 'You lot must have planted it there!'

DC Kennedy just looked at Peter and smiled. 'I've never heard that one before, have you Barry?' he asked the driver who looked in the rear mirror and laughed.'

'Is that all you've got?' said the driver. 'The DCI will love you. Oh, how I'd love to be a fly on the wall when you him tell that one! Will you be there Colin?'

'No, it'll be DS O'Neill and DCI Morrison,' he replied.

'What happened to DI Redding? I thought she was leading on this case?'

'She was until she messed up so the DCI has taken over.'

'Oh really, what did she do?'

'Not in front of him,' said Colin nodding towards Peter. 'I'll tell you later Barry!'

'Oh, of course,' said Barry, feeling a little foolish for asking.

Peter was pleased to hear that Claire was off the case and hadn't been involved with his arrest. *That would explain why she couldn't intervene,* he thought. *But it didn't explain why his alibi had been dismissed so readily. She had given him the clear impression that everything would be fine but everything was not fine.* His mind went back to small bag. *How on earth did it get there?* None of it made any sense to Peter.

Chapter 31

10:45 am: Friday, 31 August 2018

Peter had been put into one of the three small interview rooms which were located along the CID corridor. A uniformed police officer was standing outside the room keeping guard. On arrival, Peter was granted permission to call his office to arrange for a solicitor. At first his boss was reluctant to help him but after hearing Peter plead his innocence he gave in and agreed to contact the legal office in Glasgow which handled all their business. Although, the legal firm specialised in commercial law they were happy to contact another branch and within ten minutes John Singleton, Solicitor, was on his way to Dumbarton to represent Peter.

Claire was sitting at her desk when Peter was put into the interview room. She was desperate to speak to him but knew if she went anywhere near him, she would be finished. She was determined to help him in any way she could but first of all she needed to find out what had happened and why he had been put under arrest. She had been under the impression that he was just being brought in for questioning given he had already volunteered an alibi for one of the burglaries. Colin and Brian had been summoned to the DCI's office and were still there. Eventually Colin came out and headed back to the incident room. Claire went after him. 'Colin, what's going on?' she asked.

DC Kennedy stopped and turned towards Claire. 'I can't say too much but we found some jewellery stashed in his kitchen. He's as guilty as sin.'

'What, you can't have. He... he couldn't have, he has an alibi.' she exclaimed.

'Does he? All we know is what he told you and let's face it, you didn't exactly go there with an open mind did you? Anyway, we haven't been able to confirm his alibi yet?'

Claire was stunned. Could she have been so wrong about a person? All through her short career she had relied on her gut instincts which had served her well up until now. She turned away from DC Kennedy, deep in thought and then stopped. 'What happened to Sally?'

'Who?'

'His dog, the Cocker Spaniel!'

'Oh, that thing, one of his neighbours took her in, said he would look after her overnight but it looks like she'll end up in the kennels. Macdonald's not going anywhere fast. As I said, he's as guilty as sin.'

Claire was determined that was not going to happen. If it came to it she would look after Sally until this mess was resolved.

Chapter 32

11:35 am: Friday 31 August 2018

John Singleton arrived at the Police Headquarters in Dumbarton within 40 minutes of the call being made. He was a wearing a well-worn grey pin stripe suit and was carrying an old tanned coloured brief case. He had worked at Carruthers, Gemmill and Watt, Solicitors, for over 30 years and was a hardened criminal lawyer who had spent most of his time in police interview rooms or court buildings defending his clients to the best of his ability. He was a no-nonsense lawyer with a low tolerance for incompetent police work and was always happy to expose bad practice to any Sheriff who was willing to listen. He had made the journey through to Dumbarton many times and knew the layout and routine of the building as well as any officer.

On arrival he was given a copy of the charge sheet containing a summary of the arrest and was briskly taken up to the interview room where he was given the chance to speak to his client before the formal police interview would commence. After hearing Peter's version of events, Singleton gave Peter some basic procedural advice on what was about to take place and cautioned him not to say anything which might harm his case. He then told the police officer outside that they were ready to commence the interview.

DCI Morrison and DS O'Neill entered the room. DS O'Neill went straight over to the digital recording system, turned it on and said, "For the purposes of the recording, Interview with Peter Macdonald of 16 Silverton Avenue, Dumbarton, held on 31 August 2018 at 11.40 am in Police Headquarters, Stirling Road, Dumbarton, in the presence of John Singleton, Solicitor, interview conducted by Detective Chief Inspector John Morrison and Detective Sergeant Brian O'Neill."

DCI Morrison commenced the interview by laying out the formal charges of theft which had been made against Peter but also advised that they would like to ask him about the deaths of Mr William Rowatt and Detective Constable Joseph Docherty which the police believed were linked to the investigation of the robberies.

Peter was stunned by the sudden revelation that he was now under suspicion of committing murder. Mr Singleton immediately responded by expressing his utmost outrage at his client only being told about this during the interview and that he had not been told in advance that this was the case.

"Mr Singleton, your client has been arrested on suspicion of committing numerous robberies in this area which may be related to one or both of these deaths. I have every right to question him on this even if you are outraged, which I very much doubt," said DCI Morrison without any hesitation. He knew exactly what he was doing and had rehearsed his response. What he found interesting though was that Macdonald was clearly shocked by his opening statement and perhaps wasn't involved in the murders after all. Nevertheless, he was determined to press on with the interview. He proceeded to ask Peter about his movements on each of the dates when the burglaries had taken place. Peter painstakingly tried to respond but given that all of the burglaries had taken place during the night, he was only able to offer a proper alibi for the one date when he was on holiday in Lake District. He reminded the DCI that he had already told DI Redding this.

At that point, DCI Morrison took out a small plastic bag which contained some jewellery and a little cloth bag. 'Do you recognise this bag?' he asked Peter.

'Yes, DC Kennedy showed it to me earlier today,' replied Peter.

'Is that right,' said the DCI. 'Can you explain why it was hidden in the cupboard under your kitchen sink then?'

'No, I can't.' said Peter beginning to get a little tired of the questioning. He wanted to say that someone must have planted it there but resisted the urge given the comments made in the car.

'Okay, has anyone else been in your house in the past few weeks?'

'No, I don't think so,' he replied and then it struck him. 'Oh, eh, yes, Claire,' he paused awkwardly, 'I mean DI Redding? She came in yesterday to ask me about the burglaries. That's when she told me about the CCTV footage and I told her I had an alibi for one of the dates.'

'So, to the best of your knowledge no one else has been in your house?'

'No.'

'So how did the bag get there? You're not suggesting that DI Redding planted it, are you?'

Peter was outraged by the suggestion. 'No, of course not! Claire would never do that to me.' Peter immediately regretted his outburst but to his surprise the DCI ignored his comment about Claire and continued questioning him.

'So, you didn't accuse a police officer of planting the bag earlier today then?' the DCI asked, knowing full well that's exactly what happened.

Singleton turned to Peter expecting him to deny it. Peter realised that he had fallen into the trap. 'Yes, I did but that was just the shock of being told it had been found in my house. I honestly have no idea how that bag got there.'

'Did you know William Rowatt?' asked DS O'Neill taking over the questioning.

'No, who is he?' asked Peter.

'He was a local fence – a dealer of stolen goods, who was found dead in his home. Where were you between 1pm and 2 pm on 28th August 2018?' asked DS O'Neil.

'Probably at work,' replied Peter.

'And where were you between 5 pm and 6 pm on 30th August?' asked the DCI.

'Probably on my way back from work; I usually finish around 5 pm and get home at about 5.45 pm depending on traffic.'

'Can anyone in your office confirm that you were working on these dates?'

'Yes, of course. Ask my boss, if you don't believe me!' exclaimed Peter.

Singleton, who was busy writing down notes on his yellow legal pad looked up and put his hand on Peter's arm to indicate that he should calm down. There was a brief pause then DS O'Neill asked, 'Do they record absence or keep a note of your movements when you're not in the office?'

'I'm sure they do. Look, why doesn't someone contact my office and get confirmation of this?'

'That's exactly what we're going to do,' replied DCI Morrison. 'We'll take a short break. Interview terminated at 11.50 am'

DS O'Neill stood up and stopped the recording. Both police officers left the room and went through to the DCI's office.

'Well, what do you think?' asked the DCI.

'I'm not sure. Did you notice his reaction when you mentioned the two deaths? He's either a brilliant actor or he's innocent.'

'Yes, he was very convincing. Can you check his movements with his office because if what he says is true then he couldn't possibly have committed the murders.'

'But not the burglaries,' said DS O'Neill. 'He can't explain how the stolen goods got into his kitchen. I'd love to see Singleton explain that one to a jury!'

The DCI laughed. 'Yes, that would be good. Okay, get in touch with his office and we'll take it from there. Won't do any harm to let him stew for a bit! Oh, you better offer them some tea or coffee, and get the jewellery down to forensics. We need to know if we can get any DNA off it. If we can match it to Macdonald then it's game over.'

'Will do,' said DS O'Neill and left the office. He approached the door of the interview room and knocked before entering as he could hear both men talking. The talking stopped as soon as he opened the door. 'Can I get you any tea or coffee?'

'Coffee please. How long is this going to take?' Singleton asked while looking at his watch. 'My client has cooperated fully and has provided two solid alibis for his whereabouts at the time of the murders.'

'I'm going to check the alibis now and then we'll see what happens," said Brian. He turned to Peter and repeated the question, 'Tea or coffee?'

'Coffee please,' said Peter.

'Right, I'll get someone to bring them in.' DS O'Neill left the room and spoke to the uniformed police officer who was standing just outside the room keeping guard.

'So what's going to happen next?' asked Peter.

'Well, providing your alibis are confirmed for the time of the murders, there's a good chance they will let you go home tonight on Police bail. You have been arrested for the burglaries and it's going to be difficult to try to explain the mystery jewellery to a jury.'

'A jury?' exclaimed Peter. 'But I'm innocent.'

'Calm down. At the moment the police have not provided any evidence that you committed the burglaries but clearly they think have a solid case for possession of stolen goods. And, now that they have you in custody, they'll try to find some forensic evidence which places you at the scene of the crimes. Don't worry, if they don't find any evidence I'll push for the burglary charges to be dropped before we get to court. You mentioned DI Redding twice during the interview. Do you know her?'

'Yes, but I don't want her to get into trouble over this,' said Peter.

'What is your relationship with her?'

'We've only just started to go out. I really like her and don't want to get her involved.'

Singleton looked down at his notes. 'You told the police that she interviewed you at your home.'

'Well, I wouldn't call it an interview. She asked me a few questions and I provided an alibi to one of the dates of the burglaries, which she accepted.'

'Okay, and were you with her the whole time during these questions?'

'Yes, wait, no I had to go upstairs to check my diary. You are not suggesting that Claire planted the jewellery while I was upstairs. No, she wouldn't. We like each other, she's not like that.'

'Well that maybe so but this is all I need to sow the seed of reasonable doubt to a jury. Don't you see, I don't need to prove she did anything, all I need to do is demonstrate that she had the opportunity to do it. In fact this might not even go to court. If I explain to DCI Morrison that I intend to introduce this in your defence he might agree to drop the charges. The last thing he'll want is to risk the suggestion of corrupt police work going public in a court room.'

'No, I don't want this. Claire could lose her job and our relationship would be finished. No. I'm instructing you as my Solicitor not to pursue this.'

Singleton sighed, 'Well, on your head be it. Let's wait and see what else the police come up with.'

Chapter 33

11:47 am: Friday 31 August 2018

DI Redding was sitting at her desk when unexpectedly the forensic report from Rowatt's house came into her email inbox; the instruction that she was now off the case had not reached the forensics team. She opened the report and then saved a copy to her hard drive. She then forwarded the email to DS O'Neill without delay thus giving the impression that she had passed it on immediately. She had a quick look around the office. Colin was the only one in the CID room at that time and he had his back to her so she took the risk of opening the report on her pc. She read through it quickly, hoping to find something that would lead to the killer but to her astonishment there was nothing. According to the report, the only DNA found on or near the body was DC Kennedy's. The small piece of material found at the window matched his jacket. She replayed the whole scene in her mind again and then something struck her.

'Colin, what route did you and Joe take when you we looking at the CCTV in town?'

'We left Dumbarton Central, walked through the Artizan Centre. I stopped to check CCTV in some of the shops on the way but Joe continued on in the direction of Rowatt's. Why do you ask?'

'Well it just occurred to me that the killer might have followed you and could be caught on camera somewhere along the route.'

DC Kennedy hesitated before responding. 'You're not supposed to be working on this case anymore or have you forgotten? Anyway, I'm way ahead of you. I have asked the Town Centre Management Company to provide copies of all recordings around about the time of death.'

'Oh, I haven't forgotten. Just trying to be helpful that's all, but it seems you are all over it anyway.' She waited a few minutes, deciding what to do next then got up and got her coat.

'Where are you going?' asked Colin.

'Just following up on a lead I've got on another case. See you later.'

'See you,' replied Colin.

Claire got in her car and headed towards the town centre. She had lied to Colin about the other case but what else was she going to say. She arrived at Dumbarton Central Train Station and parked her car on Station Road. She had decided to follow the route that the two detectives had followed in an attempt to piece together what might have happened to Joe.   She noticed the cash generator store that Colin had visited the night before and went in.

Having briefly introduced herself to the store manager she quickly established that DS Kennedy had been in yesterday and had looked at the CCTV recordings.   She asked to see the same footage which Colin had viewed and could see nothing of any value.   When she came out, she noticed the Ladbrokes betting shop across the other side of the pedestrianised walkway.   She entered the small betting shop and asked to speak to the Manager.

A small middle aged man with greying hair came out of the back office and introduced himself. Hello, he said. 'I'm John Baxter, Manager. How can I help?'

Claire quickly introduced herself and showed her ID. "I'm investigating the murder of Bill Rowatt.'

'Oh yes, I heard about that, terrible business. Bill was a nice guy.'

'You knew him then?' asked Claire.

The man nodded his head, 'Bill was a regular customer, we'll really miss him and his money.' he said smiling at his little joke.

'In that case, I'd like to have a look at your CCTV recordings.'   Claire could see there were several cameras placed around the room.   'How long do you keep the recordings?' she asked.

'We usually keep it for a week then we overwrite the disk and start again. What date do you want to look at?'

'Didn't DC Kennedy ask to see your CCTV footage yesterday?' she asked.

'Who? Oh you mean Colin, haven't seen him for a couple of days.'

'What do you mean?'

'He's a regular customer too.'

Claire remembered the conversation between Colin and Brian about going to the bookies to bet on a hot tip. 'Of course, well can I have a look at your CCTV?'

'Sure, come round the back hen and I'll get one of my staff to help you.'

She hated being referred to as 'hen' but DI Redding said nothing and followed the small man through a side door and into the back office. She spent over an hour reviewing the CCTV which turned out to be quite revealing. She took a copy of the recordings that interested her and headed back to her car. Just as she was about to open her car door, a man wearing a black balaclava over his face approached her from behind and hit her on the back of the head with a short wooden baton. DI Redding blacked out immediately and collapsed in a heap. The man caught her as she fell and then dragged her into the open boot of his car. He dumped her body in the boot, closed it quickly and looked around to see if anyone had seen him. Satisfied that he had gotten away with it, he drove off at high speed. He knew he had to get rid of her very quickly if he was going to get away with this and headed towards the Bowling basin; a deep inset of water where the Bowling canal merged with the River Clyde.   He intended to dump the unconscious body into the cold water and weigh it down with some old bricks so it would be a while before it was discovered. He left the A82 at the Bowling roundabout and drove towards the Bowling Basin. He turned into a small road which led down to the river and found a quiet spot which he hoped couldn't be seen from the main road. He stopped the car, put on the balaclava and got out the car looking around as he did so. He couldn't see anyone and decided to open the boot. Just as the boot opened he felt the full force of Claire's right shoe under his chin. She had woken up and managed to position herself with her back on the floor and her knees up to her chin waiting for her kidnapper to open the boot. Her timing was perfect; the heal of her shoe drove the man's chin straight up, crushing his jaw, breaking his teeth lifting him off the ground. It was his turn to black out.

Chapter 34

12:59 pm: Friday 31 August 2018

When the man in the balaclava came round he was lying on the river bank face down with both hands cuffed behind his back. Claire was sitting on the rear bumper of the small car holding a blood soaked handkerchief firmly on the gash on the back of her head. She could hear the sirens of police cars approaching the Basin from the main road. She still felt a bit woozy from the blow to the head and felt like she was going to throw up.

The first police car arrived just as Claire thought she was going to pass out. DS O'Neill jumped out of the car and immediately ran to her assistance. He could see she was distressed. 'Claire, are you okay?'

Claire just stared at her rotund colleague who was looking particularly dishevelled, with shirt hanging out of his ill-fitting trousers and tie half way round his neck.

'Sorry, stupid question,' he said. 'Paramedics are on their way so just sit tight.' He turned and looked at the thief who was lying groaning on the ground. Brian went over to him and bent down. He lifted the balaclava over the man's head. 'What the...Colin?' Brian looked at Claire, who just nodded in response.

'He's the thief and the killer. I've got...' before she could finish her sentence she dropped to the ground. DS O'Neill immediately ran over to her. He turned towards the other police officers who were now approaching the scene and shouted, 'Get a paramedic now!'

Chapter 35

3:10 am: Saturday 1 September 2018

Claire woke up in a hospital bed. She could hear voices but her vision was blurred. As she came round she could start to make out a few of the faces standing round her.

'Hi Brian,' she said to her colleague who was talking to a young female doctor at the end of the bed.'

He turned towards Claire and smiled, 'How are you feeling boss? We were all a bit worried there for a while.'

'My head's a bit sore and my vision's a bit blurry but otherwise I feel okay.'

The young doctor approached the side of her bed. 'Hello, I'm Doctor Fraser. You're in the Royal Alexandria Hospital, Paisley. You've had a bad blow to your head and have a bad case of concussion so I'm afraid we'll need to keep you here for a day or two for observation. We've stitched up the wound which is all under the hairline so won't be a problem long term. You'll need to take care brushing your hair for a while though. Don't want to disturb the stitches! Oh and your parents are here; they have been here all night.'

'All night? How long have I been out?' Claire asked.

'About 14 hours in all but we gave you a sedative before we put you in the scanner which has helped you to sleep.'

'A scanner, I don't remember that!' exclaimed Claire.

'It's okay, we wouldn't expect you to remember much when under sedation. Do you remember what happened yesterday?'

'Oh, yes. Brian, where's Colin?'

He turned and looked towards the young doctor who read his signal. 'I'll leave you two to chat but not for too long, she needs to rest,'

'Understood,' Brian replied.

'Right. I'll let your parents know that you are fully conscious so don't be long as they are very anxious to see you.'

Claire smiled at the young doctor. 'Thank you, we'll not be long, promise.'

Doctor Fraser nodded, turned and left the two officers to speak.

Brian spoke first. 'Colin's on the fourth floor recovering from surgery. You really did some job on him.'

'Served him right; he was going to dump me in the river. If I hadn't woken up I'd be a goner.'

'Well, thank goodness you did. Anyway, we will need to take a full statement from you as soon as you're up for it. I'm desperate to find out how you worked out it was Colin. I still can't believe it.'

'I know and to be honest I still wasn't sure until he attacked me. There's some interesting footage on the CCTV recording which I have in my bag.' She paused. 'My bag! Where's my bag?'

'It's okay. We have it in evidence.'

'That's a relief! Anyway, I'll explain everything and give you a full statement after I've seen my parents. My mother will be going bananas in that waiting room so better let them see that I'm fine so they can go home and stop worrying.'

'Parents never really stop worrying do they? I'll go and get them.'

'Wait, what happened to Peter?' she asked anxiously.

'He was let out on police bail last night. I got in touch with his work and they confirmed that he was working at the time of the two killings. We also managed to confirm the alibi he gave to you about one the burglaries. The DCI still thinks he's involved in some way so he hasn't dropped all the charges yet but to be fair, all we have to go on at the moment is your accusation that Colin is the thief and killer. We really need your full statement.'

'You'll get it. Does Peter know I'm here?'

'We wouldn't normally share that type of information with a civilian,' said Brian one eye winking at Claire.

'Okay, you better go and get my parents, and thanks Brian. You're a good friend.'

'And you're a bloody good cop.'

'Thanks, but listen, you have known Colin for a lot longer than I have so it would have been harder for you to even think he might have been capable of being the thief, never mind a killer.'

'How did you work it out?'

'Do you remember the conversation we had with Mrs Daly, who lived opposite Rowatt?' she asked.

'How could I forget!' he said. 'I've still got the smell of that flat up my nose.'

Claire smiled, trying hard not to laugh as her head felt it would explode. 'Well, something bothered me about what she said. She said she looked out of the window at approx. 2 p.m. and confirmed that she saw Colin.'

Brian nodded slowly not quite sure where this was going.

'Our focus was on identifying the killer and how he managed to get way without being seen. We concluded that he must have left by the back window and escaped through the garden.'

Brian nodded in agreement. 'Yes, and that still makes sense.'

It was Claire's turn to nod. 'Yes, it does, but what I missed at the time was how did Colin manage to get there so quickly if he was supposed to be keeping an eye on one of the other dealers on the list? You called him at about 2 pm but Mrs Daly actually said she had seen Colin's car at that time. We both assumed she had just got the timing wrong as Colin had told us he arrived at Rowatt's at ten past two but it turns out she wasn't wrong after all. Colin lied to us about the time to put us off his scent!'

'I can't believe it. How could I have been so stupid!'

'No Brian, not stupid. We both ignored the obvious because it would never occur to us that the thief could be one of our own. Why would we question the word of a police officer over an elderly lady who appeared to be slightly confused?'

DS O'Neill nodded in agreement. 'Of course, and when I called Colin and told him that we knew that Rowatt was the dealer, he panicked. He knocks the front door and Rowatt, who doesn't suspect anything, lets him in. The door is locked and Colin decides the only way to protect himself is to kill poor Rowatt. He then breaks the window at the rear of the property to make it look like the killer broke in via the window and then makes his way to the front of the house and returns to his car. We arrived and the rest is history.'

'Yes, but he gets even luckier. I instruct him to enter the house from the rear window which means that when we find Colin's DNA on the body, which the forensic report confirmed by the way, we are not surprised by this.'

'How did you see the report,' and then the penny dropped. 'You copied the report before sending it to me. You little devil.'

'Yes, and that is when I worked it all out. It explained everything. Colin, with his police background and training would know how to avoid making most of the mistakes made by common thieves, but much worse than that, he had access to all the evidence. He could hide anything which put suspicion his way. I bet if we take a closer look at the case files we'll be able to find evidence of tampering. Oh yes, it all makes sense now. That explains why he was so keen to review the CCTV. It was the perfect opportunity for him to cover up any trace of the real thief being caught on camera but not only that he finds an innocent suspect to put us off the trail but this time he is not so lucky. He points the blame at Peter Macdonald who just happens to have a dog.'

'It still doesn't explain how the jewellery ended up in Peter's house though.' said Brian.

'That's easy, but actually quite brilliant. Colin knows I'm seeing Peter and he knew I was going to interview him after work so he follows me there. He sees Peter and Sally and knows that at some point Peter will take Sally out for a walk. He waits until the house is empty, picks the lock to the back door, enters the kitchen and plants the jewellery under the sink. Simples!' said Claire mimicking the irritating meerkat which sells insurance on the television.

'Of course, it's so flipping obvious. And you are so right. I couldn't see through any of it because it was Colin. Anyway, enough of me wallowing in self-pity, I'd better let you see your parents and I'd better phone the DCI. He's going to love this! Not!!' I'll be back later to take a full statement.'

'No problem, see you later,' said Claire as she watched Brian head off to find her parents. She was beginning to feel a bit better now. It was good to share her theory with Brian but she knew the job was only half done. They would now need to prove that Colin was the thief and a killer. They had him for kidnapping and assault of a police officer which was serious enough but he deserved to go down for a very long time. She thought about Joe and started to weep a little just as her Mum and Dad came into her room. She rubbed her eyes and smiled at her two parents.

'Hi Mum, hi Dad,' she said.

Her Mum immediately came over to hug her. 'How are you sweetheart? You gave us a real fright, didn't she dad?'

'Yes, you certainly did. Your mother has been driving the nursing staff up the wall trying to get answers.'

'Well, as you can see, I'm fine. The doctor said the scan was clear and I'm just concussed. They'll keep me in for a few days, just for observation, and then I'll be good to go.'

'Claire, maybe now is not the best time to talk about this but are you sure you're cut out to be a police officer?' said her Mum looking at her Dad for support.

'You're right Mum, now is not the time. I love my job and I'm good at it and this incident doesn't change a thing.'

It was her Dad's turn to respond. 'It's not fair you know, putting your Mum and me through this. We worry about you, all the time, and then this happens. We get a call that you've been rushed to hospital and no one can tell us what happened and if you're going to be okay. It's not easy you know.'

Claire mellowed a little. 'Look, I'm sorry but you shouldn't worry. I'm more than capable of looking after myself. You should see the other guy!'

Claire's Dad gave a wry smile 'That's my girl.'

'John Redding, she doesn't need any encouragement from you,' snapped Claire's Mum. She always used his proper name when giving him a row.

Claire's parents moved off the subject of police work and chatted for a while before heading home, happy in the knowledge that their only daughter was safe.

Brian came back accompanied by another PC and took a full statement from Claire. She told him more about what she had discovered at the betting shop. When she had checked their records it was clear that Colin had been a regular gambler but every now again he would turn up with large quantities of cash. As Brian was about to leave he promised Claire that he would keep her up to date with developments and was confident that when the DCI read her statement he would drop all charges against Peter.   Claire, tired from giving the statement, thanked Brian, laid back in her bed and drifted slowly off to sleep.

Chapter 36

2.35 pm: Saturday, 1 September 2018

DC Colin Kennedy was lying in a hospital bed when he regained consciousness. He had undergone surgery on his face and was feeling a little groggy from the anaesthetic. When he tried to lift his left arm up he realised that it was handcuffed to the bedframe. His other arm was free but was attached to a drip; a small needle had been inserted in one of the big veins in his arm. He looked around the small private room which had its own TV and WC.

There was a police officer sitting at the far end of the room, who was chatting to someone on his mobile phone. 'No, I'm upstairs with Kennedy. You should see the state of his face – wires everywhere. DI Redding, no I haven't see her yet. She's down in another ward on the first floor I think. She's okay but is being kept in for concussion. DS O'Neill spoke to her earlier and said she was *compos mentis* despite the gash on her head. Me? I'm here until 8 pm then I'm off. Okay mate, I'll see you down the pub for a beer after the shift.' The young policeman stood up and walked over to the large window at the end of the room. He stretched his arms out wide, yawned and return to the chair at the foot of the bed.

Kennedy could feel the steel pins which had been placed in his jaw to hold the various breaks in place while it healed. The pain soon turned to anger as he replayed the scene at Bowling over and over again in his head. He was determined that she would pay for this. If Redding hadn't taken on the case he would never have been caught. He decided there and then that he would pretend he was still sleeping and then when the opportunity arose, he would break out of the ward and pay DS Redding a visit she would never forget. He regretted killing Joe but had no choice. The Town Centre CCTV would prove conclusively that Rowatt arrived home just before 2.00 pm on the day he died and this time he would not be able to cover it up as Joe had made it clear that he would help him review it. 'Two heads were better than one,' Joe had said. Kennedy knew if that happened it was only a matter of time before the DI would connect the dots and come to the conclusion that he had to be the killer. So he had decided to kill DC Docherty in order to ensure that he could cover up the CCTV evidence. He had thought he was high and dry when Macdonald had been arrested and the DCI had told Redding that she was off the case but she just wouldn't let go and so he knew he would need to kill her but that hadn't worked out the way he had planned it and now here he was lying in a hospital bed with a broken jaw and facing a life sentence.

He didn't have to wait too long for his opportunity. After less than an hour, he heard his police guard get up from his seat, walk around the bed, check if Kennedy was okay and then went into the small toilet. Kennedy quickly rolled over onto his side where his arm was handcuffed, he used the thumb and forefinger on his left hand to remove the small needle from his arm and then took it with his free hand. Within 5 seconds he had unpicked the handcuff. He could hear the tap water running as the young police officer started to wash his hands and knew he had to act quickly. He grabbed a visitor chair and wedged it hard between the door handle and the floor trapping the young police officer inside the toilet.

Kennedy moved towards the door at the far end of the small room and slowly opened the handle. He quickly looked up and down the corridor to see if anyone was watching and then walked smartly toward the stairwell which he knew would lead to the lower floors. He felt pleased with himself that he had executed the plan so well and had escaped with such ease but more importantly he would now be able to release the rage inside him.

Chapter 37

3:00 pm: Saturday, 1 September 2018

When DS O'Neill returned to the station, he decided it was only fair to call Peter to let him know that Claire was conscious and was able to receive visitors. Peter decided to visit Claire that afternoon. He asked Mr Fraser if he would look after Sally again for a few hours. Mr Fraser was more than happy to help after Peter had explained what had happened.

When Peter arrived at the hospital he went straight up to the first floor where he had been told that he would find Claire. He entered the corridor and immediately went to the nurses' station where he was directed to DI Redding's room. He opened the door and could not believe what he was seeing. At first he thought there was a doctor attending to Claire but he very quickly realised that something was wrong.

'Hey, what's going on? What are you doing?' shouted Peter enraged at what he was seeing. He ran over and grabbed the man's shoulder firmly and pulled at him. To his horror the man turned his head to expose his face full of metal wires. Peter recognised the man to be DC Kennedy and flinched at the grotesque sight. This allowed Kennedy to stand up quickly, turn and swing his right arm at Peter connecting with his chin and knocking him sideways onto the floor. Kennedy, who wasn't wearing any shoes, proceeded to stamp on Peter with the sole of his right heel. Peter had no option but to try to defend himself with his arms but was no match for the powerful stamping action of his attacker. After taking a few heavy blows to the face and upper body Peter decided he had to change tactics and grabbed the man's foot. He got a firm grip and managed to get to his feet at the same time raising the man's foot above his waist level throwing him off balance and then falling to floor. This time Peter had the upper hand and decided to return the damage which had been inflicted on him. However, he had the advantage of wearing hard soled shoes. Just as Kennedy tried to get back up Peter kicked him hard on the jaw. The explosion of pain inflicted on the already broken jaw was too much for Kennedy's brain to cope with and he blacked out. He fell backwards onto the floor next to Claire's bed and lay there in a heap.

As all this was happening Claire started to come round a little and starting coughing a few times to clear her throat.

'Are you okay Claire. Sit there, don't move and I'll get a nurse. Wait, no, I'm not leaving you with him.' Peter leaned over the hospital bed and pressed the red emergency button. Within seconds a young nurse followed by another older nurse came into the room and were shocked to see the Kennedy's body lying on the floor.

'He's unconscious, I think,' said Peter. 'That maniac tried to kill Claire, he was trying to strangle her.'

One of the nurses took charge. 'Jackie, call the police, now, I think there's an officer on the fourth floor.' She then went over to Claire. 'Are you okay?'

'I am now thanks, thought I was a goner there but thankfully Peter intervened in the nick of time,' Claire replied.

Kennedy started to groan and move. Peter, realising that the danger wasn't quite over leaped over to where Kennedy was lying on the floor, he turned him over and grabbed his left arm and twisted it behind his back and then sat on him. Kennedy was pinned to the floor and despite struggling couldn't move with the weight of Peter's body. He started to shout at Peter to get off and spat blood onto the floor from his bleeding mouth. Within a few minutes, the police officer who had been guarding Kennedy came rushing into the room. 'Is everyone alright? The bugger managed to trap me in the toilet. I don't know how he escaped; he must have picked the lock on the handcuffs.'

'It's okay,' said Claire in an attempt to calm the young police officer who was clearly in a bit of a panic. 'You'd better cuff both his hands this time and take him back upstairs. I have a feeling he might need some more surgery.'

Kennedy groaned as the young police officer handcuffed him and helped him get to his feet. He glared at Peter who was now on his feet standing by the door. Peter stood back and opened the door to let the two men out of the room. He then went over to Claire. 'Are you really alright?'

'Well, my head hurts and my neck hurts but apart from that I'm absolutely brand new.' she said smiling.

Peter smiled back at Claire. 'Well, at least you haven't lost your sense of humour.'

The nurse, who had been sitting quietly throughout the scene approached the bed. 'Sorry to interrupt but I think the doctor will need to examine you again. Just to be sure.'

'Of course,' said Claire. 'But give me a few minutes with Peter alone, okay.'

'Sure, I'll go and look for him. He won't be on the ward during visiting hour anyway so I'll need to call him. I'll be back in a few minutes.'

'Thanks,' said Claire.

'Peter, I want you to know that I never for a minute thought that you were guilty. I'm sorry the DCI put you through all that. I tried…'

Peter cut her off, 'It's okay Claire, DS O'Neill explained everything when he called to tell me you were okay. He also told me that you singlehandedly caught the thief or should I say killer. I guess that was him then?'

'Yes, that was him. It's a good thing you stopped him. I must have been sleeping when he came in, he already had a good grip on me before I realised what was happening. I really thought I was going to die.'

Peter eyes started to well up with tears. He had never felt this way about anyone before and he knew there and then that she was the one for him..

Claire looked into his eyes and could read his mind. 'Oh come here you big softy,' she said reaching out to him for a hug.

He hugged her back, holding her tight promising himself he would never let her go. He could feel her tears on his neck as the emotion of the moment overcame them both.

The young doctor opened the door opened without knocking and entered the room. 'Oops, sorry,' he said.

Claire opened her tear filled eyes. 'It's okay,' she said letting Peter go and wiped her eyes with the cuff of her gown sleeve.

Peter released his hold and turned to face the doctor. 'I'd better leave you to it, 'I'll be back tomorrow to see you Claire, he said softly and kissed her on the cheek. He left the room, his heart bursting with joy.

As he walked down the corridor, he was approached by DS O'Neill who had been told about the incident and had broken all the speed limits to get to the hospital as fast as he could. Peter told him that the doctor was with Claire and gave him a brief statement on his fight with DC Kennedy. DS O'Neill thanked him for taking on Kennedy and told Peter that he might need to interview him again if needed any more information. Peter confirmed that he was happy to do so and walked towards the exit.

Chapter 38

8:30 pm: Saturday, 1 September 2018

Peter was upstairs when he heard a loud knock on the door which was the trigger for Sally to start barking. Peter went downstairs and opened the door to see DCI Morrison and DS O'Neill waiting patiently.

'Sorry to appear so late in the day,' said DCI Morrison. 'Can we come in and have a chat?'

Peter was a bit taken back by the presence of the DCI. 'Sure, come on in. I'll just put Sally in the kitchen. Come on girl,' he said as he led Sally into the small kitchen to the rear of the property and then closed the door.

When he came back, the two men had come into the house and were standing in the narrow hallway.

'Come on into the living room and have a seat," said Peter leading the way.

DCI Morrison took a deep breath before speaking. 'We're here to thank you for what you did in the hospital today and to apologise for any inconvenience we caused you yesterday. We now know you're not the thief and have dropped all charges.'

Peter relaxed into his chair. 'Thank goodness for that. You had me a bit worried there!'

'Sorry about that,' replied DCI Morrison.

DS O'Neill explained what had happened. 'We carried out a full search of DC Kennedy's home and found a small black rucksack that contained some interesting tools, but more importantly we also found some items of jewellery which we are confident will match some of the items stolen from recent burglaries. We also know that DC Kennedy had a second car which we believe he used to travel to and from the scenes of crime. As chance would have it, DC Kennedy had been tasked with looking at all the CCTV recordings relating to the burglaries so he was able to overlook the presence of his car but worse than that he used the CCTV to falsely identify you as our main suspect. We now believe he was the one who planted the stolen jewellery in your kitchen, which resulted in your arrest.'

'Yes, but trying to frame you for this was his biggest mistake.' said the DCI taking over the conversation. 'He might have managed to fool the rest of us but not DI Redding who knew you were innocent. As I said earlier, we can only apologise for the distress we have caused you; taking you out of your office, creating a scene at your home and so on. If it helps, I'll call your boss first thing on the Monday morning and explain everything.'

'That's very decent of you. I'm just relieved it's all over and you've got him now,' said Peter.

'Well thanks to you and Di Redding he's still in hospital under police custody and he won't escape again, I've made sure of that,' said DCI Morrison getting to his feet.

He offered his hand to Peter who stood up to accept the handshake. The two policemen left the small house watched by Peter who waved them off from his doorstep. He went into the kitchen and let Sally out. 'Come on Sally, I've still got some work to do and then I'll take you for a long walk. He went upstairs smiling to himself. *If only they knew.*

After a few months of working as a stockbroker, Peter had discovered that there was plenty of money to be made buying and selling stocks and shares, especially if you ran your own little business from the comfort of your own home. Yes, he made a good living from his day job but there was more money to be made by using other people's funds to make a profit for himself and not his firm. At night, he would sit upstairs in his makeshift office buying and selling shares from markets all around the world; they operated at different hours from the UK which suited him to a tee. He had created his own online shares company which attracted small investors from all over the world but he never accepted any from the UK; that was too risky. He also didn't take any risks with the buying and selling of shares and had made a lot of money for his clients over the years. They would never know that he had skimmed their profits by artificially inflating the purchase price of any shares purchased. And, on the odd occasion when he had made a loss he would simply pass the whole amount onto his clients, but still take the commission for the transaction; he just couldn't lose. He was careful with the money he made; most of it was banked off shore where the tax man couldn't reach it. It really was the perfect crime and the only luxury that he afforded himself was the new BMW that he had purchased five years ago. Ever since he was a child he had dreamed of owning such a car. It was a reminder that despite everything that life had thrown at him as a child, he had made it. However, more importantly, Peter had decided that now was the time to stop. He had plenty of money and his relationship with Claire was too important to him to risk so, without any reservation, he had decided to end his little business venture and shut down the website for good. He still had a few lose ends to tidy up but he was ready to start a new life and put his past behind him.

About the Author and the Book

Andrew Hawthorne is married, has three children and lives and works in Scotland. He started writing in 2018 in an attempt to inspire his youngest son to write stories. He has written four children's stories in addition to this, his debut novel.

None of the characters in the book are real but all of the buildings, place names, directions, and street names are accurate. The 'L' Division Police HQ (referred to as a concrete monstrosity in the book) is still in use and can be seen from the A82 as you pass through Dumbarton. However, its neighbouring concrete monstrosity which was known locally as 'the County Buildings' in which the author worked for over 30 years, has since been demolished and replaced with an ultra-modern new office complex in the centre of Dumbarton.

Andrew's second book, The Keeper (book 2 in the DI Redding series was published in November 2021).

Printed in Great Britain
by Amazon

80704819R10102